DING DONG DEAD

DING DONG DEAD

DEB BAKER

WHEELER
CHIVERS

This Large Print edition is published by Wheeler Publishing, Waterville, Maine, USA and by BBC Audiobooks Ltd, Bath, England.
Wheeler Publishing, a part of Gale, Cengage Learning.
The text of this Large Print edition is unabridged.
Other aspects of the book may vary from the original edition.
Set in 16 pt. Plantin.
Printed on permanent paper.

LIBRARY OF CONGRESS CATALOGING-IN-PUBLICATION DATA

Baker, Deb, 1953–
  Ding dong dead / by Deb Baker.
    p. cm. — (Wheeler large print cozy mystery)
  ISBN-13: 978-1-59722-961-6 (softcover : alk. paper)
  ISBN-10: 1-59722-961-X (softcover : alk. paper)
  1. Birch, Gretchen (Fictitious character)—Fiction. 2. Dolls—Collectors and collecting—Fiction. 3. Murder—Investigation—Fiction. 4. Large type books. I. Title.
  PS3602.A586D56 2009
  813'.6—dc22   2009001969

BRITISH LIBRARY CATALOGUING-IN-PUBLICATION DATA AVAILABLE

Published in 2009 in the U.S. by arrangement with The Berkley Publishing Group, a member of Penguin Group (USA) Inc.
Published in 2009 in the U.K. by arrangement with The Berkley Publishing Group, a member of Penguin Group (USA) Inc.

U.K. Hardcover: 978 1 408 44172 5 (Chivers Large Print)
U.K. Softcover: 978 1 408 44173 2 (Camden Large Print)

Baker, Deb, 195

Ding dong dead
/ Deb Baker

Printed in the United States of America
1 2 3 4 5 6 7 13 12 11 10 09

LP

1811765

DING DONG DEAD

1

Doll museums can be found in the most unlikely places. Doll shop owners know how to locate the museums that aren't publicly advertised. Shops tend to be family affairs. Grandma might have been a serious collector who had a private collection on display for friends and family. You never know when a door will open and you will have the opportunity to view a rare and valuable museum-quality collection.

— From *World of Dolls* by Caroline Birch

Gretchen Birch looked down at the ten-card spread, wishing her aunt had chosen a different preoccupation. Nina wore a head scarf for dramatic effect. "You drew all bardo cards!" she whispered in her husky voice. "Out of a deck of seventy-eight tarot cards, only thirteen of them are negative. How could this happen?"

Nina stared at the cards, worry creased on

her forehead.

Gretchen glanced over at the contemporary doll reference book she had been using to research a one-of-a-kind Shirley Temple. That was before Nina had burst into her workshop with her tiny diva dog, Tutu, and distracted Gretchen from her real work. She was a doll restoration artist and needed to restyle a unique Shirley Temple doll's hair exactly as it had been in the 1930s. The customer expected the doll back today.

Nina cleared her voice. "You are in imminent danger unless you overcome external influences. The cards show despair and futility!"

Despair. Futility.

Gretchen glanced sharply across the table at her aunt. Old-fashioned words coming from the New Age queen.

"Your unconscious mind picked the cards," Aunt Nina said. "You can't blame me."

The tarot deck illustrated full scenes, complete with figures and symbols. Gretchen's ten cards, all faceup, depicted steely swords and women wearing blindfolds, their arms pinned to their sides with bindings. Had Gretchen believed in this stuff, she would have been concerned. She pointed at one of the cards. "Three swords slicing through a red heart. What does that mean?"

"Sorrow and strife. It's your final outcome card, the results of the other influences, and your destiny, if you don't change your path."

Wobbles, Gretchen's companion cat, stretched out on the sofa, watching the two women. The black tomcat was missing a back leg, consequences of a hit-and-run car accident, but he had adapted well to his disability. He stared at Gretchen without blinking.

"Aren't you supposed to give me positive guidance?" Gretchen asked. "This is all doom and gloom."

"I'm only the interpreter. I can't help it that you selected negative cards."

"Can we reshuffle?"

Nina shook her head. "No. See this?" She held up a card. "The nine of wands. This card means you have a hidden enemy. My advice is to quit your present path."

"How do I do that?"

"Don't do the museum project, or at least turn it over to someone else."

"I can't do that." The Phoenix Dollers Club was hard at work on a luncheon and play presentation to benefit a house that they were converting into a museum, an unexpected opportunity they couldn't pass up. "We've started rehearsals," Gretchen

9

said. "The play must go on."

"I can't force you, of course. You've always been willful. But I'm warning you, Gretchen. Don't take a passive approach to your life. You can change your future."

Aunt Nina had come a long way with her readings. Last month she'd still been using an instruction booklet. She didn't need it any longer. "After the information presented in these cards, I'll have to stay close by and protect you from yourself."

"I'm a big girl, Nina."

"Even big girls make mistakes." She held up one of the other cards on the table.

"The nine of swords," Gretchen's aunt said. "Misfortune! Ruin! Pain!"

2

May Day. May 1. Instead of dancing around a maypole with multicolored ribbons streaming behind her, Gretchen was crouched on the rough ground, surrounded by desert shrubs and cacti. Yet in spite of her surroundings, Gretchen felt like the May Queen.

"There," Matt said, squatting on the ground next to her. The wonderful and familiar aroma of his Chrome cologne wafted through the air. "That's the spot." She heard excitement in his voice. She was right there with him, feeling it, too.

She could think of worse things than spending the final hour right before dusk on the hard earth of Phoenix's Camelback Mountain beside the man she'd been lusting after. Not that she would ever admit to lusting. But she was.

In fact, she was lusting this very minute. Three months into their relationship and they still were performing the opening act of the mating ritual, as they had agreed. First-base kid stuff. Both of them were recovering from bad relationships; Gretchen from discovering that her longtime lover had a fidelity problem, Matt from a marriage to an unfaithful wife that had ended in a messy divorce. They had agreed to take it slowly, not rush into anything too intimate.

Slow was okay with Gretchen, but according to Nina this was getting ridiculous. "You're adults," she'd said. "Not teenagers. Lose the clothes." At the moment, lying prone next to Matt on a secluded ridge on the mountain, Gretchen agreed with her aunt.

She should be savoring every moment of the romance, all the richness and wonderfully complex emotions that go with it. Instead, the sexual tension was growing between them every day. Matt had to be feeling it, too, but it wasn't a subject she felt comfortable discussing with him.

They had taken to crawling around on mountains, observing the mating habits of other species. Not exactly the best solution to built-up frustration.

"Right there," Matt said.

Gretchen looked in the direction he indicated, getting her bearings before leveling the binoculars. She gasped involuntarily as she trained the lenses on a mesquite bush and found it. Yes. Another bird to add to her growing life list.

A male phainopepla — shiny black with a long tail and a tall crest, just like the picture in her bird book.

"Wheeda-lay," it called.

The female flew in and landed next to her partner.

A couple, like Matt and Gretchen. A pair. After the final heart-wrenching discoveries before her fiancé became her ex, she was staying cautiously optimistic.

Gretchen could see the female phainopepla's signature red eyes. "How do you pronounce the name again?" She was a better climber than Matt, but he knew his birds and their calls.

"Fay-no-PEP-la. Do you see both of them?"

"Yes." Still holding the binoculars to her eyes, she watched the pair take off together as though on cue.

"Did you see the white patch on top of the wing?"

"Yes."

Gretchen lowered the binoculars. Matt wasn't watching the birds fly off. He was gazing steadily at her. He flashed a smile.

The guy had the best smile in the world. "Come here," he said, sitting down and reaching out to her.

She scooted over and they kissed under an enormous saguaro cactus, its white flowers closed since late afternoon. After nightfall they would open again. The romantic in Gretchen wanted to stay, watch them reopen, let nature take its course.

"I know what you're thinking," Matt said.

"Really?" She hoped not.

"Let me show you."

The second kiss should have been sweeter than the first, but instead Gretchen felt the familiar and highly annoying vibration of his cell phone.

Matt released her abruptly and raised the phone to his ear. "Detective Albright," he said, suddenly all business.

Gretchen sat up straight and allowed herself an internal moan. She wanted to throw his phone off a cliff. She was used to long hours spent apart from Steve, her ex-fiancé. He was an attorney, driven to make partner, but Matt's career as a Phoenix detective seemed to consume him even more. His work cut into the tiny amount of time they found for each other. It would take some getting used to.

She saw the hard edge to his jaw, the narrowing eyes. She could feel the distance between them growing as it always did when he switched into work mode.

Just great. Here it comes.

"Gotta go," he said, snapping the phone closed and rising. "I'm sorry."

"Me, too."

They began the descent, Matt moving faster than she thought safe.

"Be careful," she warned, hopping from rock to rock. "Don't slip."

"As soon as we're in the car, call your mother. Ask her to pick you up at Eternal View Cemetery. I'll be busy for the rest of the night."

Stones gave way under his feet.

"Slow down," she warned again.

Amateurs! They thought the hardest part of a mountain climb was the ascent, but beginners suffered more injuries on the way back down by becoming too relaxed, too careless. Gretchen took a final moment to look out over the Sonoran Desert, at the city of Phoenix spread out below. She slowed to take it in and to consider lost possibilities and opportunities.

If only she'd destroyed his phone.

"Hurry up, please." Matt kept going.

"All right. I'm coming. Tell me what happened."

"A homicide."

"In Eternal View Cemetery?"

"Yes."

Gretchen glanced at Matt, taking in his broad shoulders and lean, muscled back. How could he do this job? And could she deal with the hours and the internal baggage that had to come with his work? Was this really what she wanted? A guy who seemed to crave danger, who mingled with drug addicts and pedophiles and killers and who knew what else?

Gretchen didn't know what the distant future held for them, but here in the present she knew she wanted Matt Albright.

Slow down, she reminded herself as they reached the trailhead, *step cautiously in this relationship in the same way you've learned to traverse rocky terrain.*

Once in his car, Gretchen attempted to reach her mother. Caroline didn't answer the home phone or her cell. Gretchen left voice messages at both locations.

Matt was on his cell phone, immersed in a world of human atrocities and blight that Gretchen hadn't been able to understand or imagine. Tonight, she would get her first chance.

Should she try to find Nina for a ride home? As soon as she thought of her aunt, she rejected the idea. Nina would flip out if she had to enter a cemetery at night, let alone one where there'd been a recent murder. Aunt Nina avoided places where negative energy lurked. One of her many quirks, right up there with her claims of colored auras and psychic messages.

Matt sped along Twenty-fourth Street and turned onto Camelback Road, heading toward the cemetery. He reached over and squeezed her shoulder, sending an electrical charge down her spine.

"I really *am* sorry," he said.

"It's okay."

"We were having such a great time."

"Wonderful," she agreed. "And I have a faynodoodad to add to my life list."

Matt laughed, but with an edge that told her he was paying only slight attention. His mind was elsewhere. "You're going to have to learn to pronounce its name properly. That's one of the most important birding rules."

"You made that up."

"On the spot."

Ahead Gretchen saw lights flashing. Matt rolled down the window when a police officer walked up to the car. Matt flipped out identification, so impatient to get to the scene that the wheels still inched forward.

"Let Caroline Birch through when she arrives," he said once the cop recognized him and waved them through.

"You're taking me inside the cemetery with you?" Gretchen had hoped he would, but hadn't expected it. He could have dropped her at the entrance to wait for her mother. Instead, she really would have the opportunity to observe him in the field.

How romantic!

"A gorgeous woman like you? The cops would be all over you. No way am I taking that chance." He flashed a quick smile. "And you know how vulnerable a woman alone is. I want you to wait in the car. Keep the doors locked until your mom gets here."

Another cop waved them through a second checkpoint.

"It happened in the old section," Matt said, driving toward the back of the cemetery. He parked behind a line of cars. A van was already positioned between the headstones, its back doors wide open. Gretchen could see a gurney inside. She looked away.

"The medical examiner beat us," he said, swinging out of the car. "Be good. Stay in the car."

He walked rapidly away before Gretchen could reply.

How was she supposed to completely understand him and his work when she was ordered to wait in the car?

Through the car's windows, Gretchen watched a flurry of activity, as much as she could make out in the darkness. People stood in a group a distance away. Two officers were with them, their heavy-duty flashlights and gleaming badges visible. Who were the others? Witnesses to the crime? Passersby who had stumbled upon a corpse? Or were they suspects?

Her cell phone rang. "I got your message," her mother said. "I'm on the way, but it's going to take about twenty minutes. Where will I find you?"

"At the crime scene."

"*What!* I don't like that at all."

"We didn't have a choice. When you get to the cemetery entrance, give your name to the officer. He'll let you through. I'm waiting in Matt's car."

"Gotcha. Oh, and Gretchen? Stay in the car."

The same thing Matt had told her.

After disconnecting, she leaned back and tried to concentrate on life rather than on death. She and her mother hadn't been particularly close until Caroline had been diagnosed with breast cancer several years

19

previously. After that, their different views on life seemed like petty reasons to continue their discord. They had established a real friendship. Caroline was a six-year cancer survivor, going on seven, and she had changed significantly. Now she pursued her dreams instead of talking about them. One of those had been writing a comprehensive doll book and seeing it published.

Alive and vibrant. Unlike the poor, dead person here tonight. Was the victim male or female? She hadn't asked.

Gretchen raised her head and peered out searching for Matt. She saw a small circle of people looking at something on the ground. A woman squatted over what must be a body. The medical examiner?

Matt wasn't in the circle. He was about thirty feet from the spot where the team worked on the body, and he was aiming a flashlight at a grave marking.

What was he looking at? Should she take one little peek to find out? She had twenty minutes before her mother would arrive. After all, she wasn't a child. Why should she wait in the car?

Gretchen slid out, closed the door as quietly as possible, and stopped behind a gravestone for a few moments. Shadows played through the cemetery, and wind

20

stirred the evergreen leaves at the top of a palm tree. She moved to the tall tree, treading quietly over the red clay earth.

The old part of the cemetery was tucked way at the back and didn't have the uniformity of the newer section. Graves weren't lined up in neatly spaced rows. Even the headstones were more varied.

She heard the murmur of voices. They reminded her of the hush of a funeral visitation, low and respectful tones. Several people bent over the deceased. No one noticed Gretchen. She crept closer to Matt, sliding along the side of the crime scene at an angle. He hadn't moved from the headstone. From her position slightly behind the detective, she could see what held his attention.

Thick writing on rough granite, the words *Die, Dolly, Die.*

All as red as the color of blood. *Please no, don't be blood,* Gretchen thought, even as she realized that it looked thicker, brighter. Lipstick? It had to be. Gretchen knew lipstick.

Matt spoke without turning around. "You were supposed to wait in the car."

Gretchen's first impulse was to duck down and crawl away. She quickly weighed the odds of retreating without making a fool of herself. They weren't good.

"How did you know it was me?" she asked.

"Mathematical deduction. Simply a matter of determining how long it would take you to disobey a direct order from a law enforcement official. By my calculations, you're right on schedule. A little behind really."

"I thought maybe I could help."

"You can help by not touching anything. Help by not getting involved."

"Okay."

"Gretchen." He stared at the grave marker. "You have a bad habit of tripping over trouble."

That was an understatement. She'd had more than her share of difficult situations recently, but she couldn't see how any of them might have been handled differently. It wasn't her fault that trouble followed her around.

"Let's not have a repeat of past disasters," he said.

"Is it lipstick?" Gretchen asked.

"Probably."

"A woman's body then?"

"Yes."

When he looked at her his face was hard and his eyes were angry. He wasn't a man she'd want to cross paths with if she had committed a murder. "The woman crawled from here over to there," he explained. The flashlight beamed along the ground between the headstone in front of them and the site where the group of professionals hovered over the body. "See those dark spots? Drops of blood."

Gretchen shuddered, staring at the ground. "What about the words?"

"Rage."

He turned and called out to the team hovering over the body. "Did you find a tube of lipstick?"

"No purse," replied the woman who Gretchen had pegged as the ME.

"How about checking the area?"

"We'll take a look," a cop said.

Gretchen stayed close to Matt.

"Can't you cooperate?" he said to her. "Can't you wait in the car like I asked?"

"I'll go in a minute." His car was parked in darkness. She needed light.

Matt's flashlight beam cast eerie shadows along the sides of the headstone. Others with flashlights were scanning the ground in the vicinity of the body. "No ID." Then the same woman's voice. "You need to see this."

"I'll be right over," Matt said.

He strode toward the murder victim's dead body. At the moment, as far as he was concerned, Gretchen had stopped existing. The intense beam from a floodlight came on, revealing more of the scene.

What are you doing? Stay back.

Gretchen ignored her inner voice and moved closer. This was her chance to understand Matt's passion. She wanted to stop feeling like she was in competition with his career. Two emergency workers partially blocked her view. They shifted positions.

The dead woman had been wearing flip-flops, but they were no longer on her feet. She wore black capris, and her white halter top was stained with blood, her long blonde hair matted with it.

So much blood, puddling on the unyielding desert floor.

Matt looked up at her. Their eyes met.

Someone else moved. Gretchen's eyes shifted back to the horror of the moment and locked onto the woman's face.

The dead woman's eyes were wide open, unblinking and unseeing.

This could have been your mother, your aunt, your friend. It could have been you!

Gretchen felt her heart pounding against her rib cage. It was purely a female thing. Fear was implanted in every woman's breast from the moment of cognitive awareness, like a pacemaker always pulsing. Be very afraid. Stay out of the dark. Don't travel alone. Be alert to danger. Carry protection and know how to use it. Learn self-defense techniques. Run fast. Scream.

The woman had made all the wrong moves and had paid the ultimate penalty.

"Gretchen," she heard behind her as she turned and fled.

She made it to the tree next to Matt's car. She leaned against the palm tree for support, fighting back waves of nausea, feeling helpless and weak against the monster that had done this to one of her kind.

When Matt reached her, she welcomed his arms, wrapped herself against his chest, and never wanted to let go.

3

Fantasy dolls are the latest rage. Unicorns, dragons, mermaids, fairies, and wizards. They are the three Ms — mystical, magical, and mysterious. For those who enjoy working with clay, creating fantasy dolls can become an addictive hobby. Kits are available for the novice enthusiast. Or dig into the clay and cast your own forms. Fantasy dolls are replicas of immortal earthly spirits with supernatural abilities. Add feathers, fibers, and fairy glitter to your newly sculpted piece and watch her come to life.

— From *World of Dolls* by Caroline Birch

Detective Terry Vascar arrives at the crime scene and parks behind a line of vehicles. Two women are greeting each other next to the car parked ahead of him. He recognizes one of them, even in the dark. It's the woman his pal Matt Albright has been dating, Gretchen Birch.

Terry swings his head and spots Matt talking to a forensics team. When he looks back, the women are moving in the opposite direction.

Terry follows, staying in the shadows, curious. They stop at a headstone, not even noticing him.

Three words appear on the marble when the younger woman shines a flashlight beam on it.

Die, Dolly, Die.

"It's not blood." Gretchen is breathing fast, rushing her words as she speaks. "It's lipstick."

A cop walks toward them, with Matt trailing behind. Terry steps in beside Matt, who nods so slightly Terry almost misses the greeting.

"Caroline," Matt says, moving forward to shake the older woman's hand. "Thanks for coming to get Gretchen."

"I don't like this."

"None of us do. Listen, we found a doll. Would the two of you take a look?"

"Of course," both women respond.

Terry watches his buddy slide away, stopping a good distance from where an officer holds up a clear bag containing a doll.

What's up with Matt?

The flashlight in Gretchen Birch's hand illuminates the doll for a moment, then swings wild, erratic. Terry takes the flashlight from her. She doesn't resist, instead giving him a look of gratitude. He shines it on the object with a steady hand.

The doll's face is exquisitely chiseled. She has long copper hair that falls to her waist. Ivy snakes up a perfectly formed leg.

A second bag contains gold wings. In the murky light, the wings sparkle like gemstone dust.

"A fantasy doll," Gretchen whispers. "Her wings have broken off."

"Yes," Caroline agrees.

"Have you seen this doll before?" Matt asks from outside the small group. "Or one like it?"

"No," Caroline says, but Terry catches something in her voice, in the startled expression on her face. Matt senses it, too, because he glances sharply at Terry.

"Thank you again, Caroline, for coming," Matt says after a pause. Terry waits while Matt escorts the women back to their car, opening doors for them and muttering reassurances. The women drive away.

"Gretchen's mother?" Terry asks.

"Yes."

"She recognized the doll."

28

"Maybe. I'll talk to her again."

Terry gestures toward the body, covered and strapped to a gurney. Strobe lights everywhere. "What's going on?"

"A murdered woman."

"Name?"

"No purse and no identification."

"But we have a doll."

"Just my luck," Matt says.

4

The man — known to his friends as Nacho, formerly called Theodore Brummer in a life he barely remembers — watches the car leave the cemetery. He thought about moving away from the group, greeting his friends Gretchen and Caroline before they drove off, but that would have called even more attention his way. The police already think he is some kind of ringleader.

Police! He hates them and their superior, suspicious attitudes.

"Vagrants," says a cop, who pretends he is doing good deeds while actually satisfying a sadist tendency to manipulate and destroy those who are weaker. He's the same one who rounded them up, flashing a club to prove his power. *Make my day. Make a move so I have an excuse to pound you into the ground.*

All Nacho wanted was a quiet place to bed down away from the dopers downtown, the addicts who will kill for a buck, for the possibility of a high. That's all any of them wanted, peace and quiet. Not this.

How could Gretchen get involved with a cop?

Here he comes, striding over like he owns the world. The one his friend Gretchen is so fond of. Albright. Nacho wants to give him the benefit of the doubt for her sake. But a cop? More benefit for him in doubt.

"Hey, Detective Albright," Nacho says. "They want to haul the lot of us in." That's what the cop had called them. *The lot,* like they aren't human. Maybe Gretchen's cop friend can help him and Daisy.

The detective nods in recognition. Good. He remembers. Nacho glances back and sees Daisy pushing forward and addressing the detective, too. "Hi," she says, friendly-like. That's Daisy, no prejudices there, even when they pick her up off the street for no good reason.

The detective honors her with another nod before consulting with the coppers, not bothering with Nacho's concern of incarceration.

Nacho doesn't want to spend the night in jail, although sleeping in a bed would be a treat. A square meal and sheets. How long has it been? He's used to passing the night in a ripped-up sleeping bag thrown down on hard desert dirt, a cover over his head if he's lucky. Black plastic sheets work when it rains. But the cops have confiscated all their possessions — Daisy's shopping cart filled with supplies, their backpacks.

Who called in the cops without warning them to leave the cemetery first? Usually Nacho is the first to know of these situations. When you live on the street, you hear it all, see it all, and you vamoose before the heat arrives. It wasn't one of theirs who made the call. That's obvious.

Too late this time. They should have gone when the going was good, when they heard the disturbance, little ripples of conflict, on the other side of the cemetery.

Detective Albright starts interrogating the clump of frightened people, asking the same questions already asked by the other cop. *Who are you? What are you doing here? What did you see go down?*

No one wants to say anything. Who would? Speak at all and they run you in and book you on some trumped up charge. None of them admits to hearing the disturbance, two people, the mutter of voices, rising, then falling, quiet after that.

There's someone whom Nacho doesn't recognize in the group. One among them doesn't belong to his community, but he isn't saying a word. He doesn't get involved in other people's business.

The streets of Phoenix are beginning to swell with more homeless people than ever before. The old-timers are forced to share more and more, make due with less all the time. No one will leave them alone. They've lost their tent city, the services they used to count on are closing up, laws are tightening, some of his acquaintances go missing by morning, rounded up and dropped off at the border. *Get out,* that's the message he hears the most. *Go someplace else.*

If he could control his drinking, he'd consider a different lifestyle. That's what Daisy hints at. A real home.

Albright gets around to the one who looks like them, but doesn't smell right. After a while, you know who fits and who doesn't. This one doesn't.

"Who are you?" Albright asks, but Nacho doesn't hear the answer because Daisy is on her cell phone. People sometimes laugh when they find out about her phone. What's a homeless person doing with a cell phone? But Daisy is amazingly secretive about her past.

Most of them don't even remember having a past. Nacho doesn't.

"We're in the cemetery," Daisy says into the phone, then listens. ". . . I don't know why . . . Didn't want to make trouble for you . . . Taking us in for questioning . . . Not yet. I'll let you know. Thanks."

Nacho thinks how cute she looks since she changed her style to that red hat thing. Daisy is wearing a floppy hat with her favorite purple dress. The rest of her wardrobe is in police custody along with everything else she owns.

"Vagrancy?" one of the cops asks the detective.

Albright replies loud enough to interrupt Nacho's eavesdropping, but that's okay, Daisy has disconnected from the call. "Book them," he hears from this man Gretchen thinks so highly of. She should be here to see how they're treated.

Nothing like joining the homeless community to realize how rotten people can be on both sides of the law.

5

The gun blast frightened all of them. Some-one screamed.

Gretchen watched with a mixture of frustration and disbelief as Bonnie dove for the floor, landing on her padded stomach. The man's black synthetic wig she wore on her head slid sideways, and her fake handle-bar mustache skidded across the floor.

Bonnie's body seized. Then her eyes stared sightlessly.

Julie Wicker dropped the weapon on the floor and covered her face with both hands. "I didn't mean to fire it," she said after clearing a space between her pinky fingers for better articulation. "It was an accident. I'm so sorry."

"Cut," Nina shouted, recovering slightly faster than Gretchen had from the unex-pected explosion. Nina stomped up to the stage to glare at the cast members. She maintained a commanding presence even while dwarfed by a six-foot Barbie mannequin dressed in a cheerleader's outfit.

"Take five," Nina ordered. "Then come back and try to do the scene the way it was written. And why did the mustache come off?"

Gretchen was the one who had applied Bonnie's mustache, another one of the many responsibilities she was trying to juggle. "Who's got the glue?" Nina continued when no one answered. "Where's makeup?"

"We do our own makeup," Bonnie said. "You know that."

Another glare from Nina. "Use superglue next time. I want that mustache to adhere so well it never comes off."

Bonnie Albright, president of the Phoenix Dollers Club and mother of the man Gretchen was dating, could have pointed an accusing finger at Gretchen, but she didn't, which raised Gretchen's esteem for the woman several notches.

Bonnie rolled to her side, pushed up into a sitting position, and readjusted her wig.

"We've been at this for hours," she griped. "We need more than a five-minute break."

The other cast members agreed.

Gretchen sighed, and followed her aunt onto the stage, picking up the blank-firing

36

revolver on the way. Not only was the cast totally inept, forgetting their lines and firing weapons at all the wrong times, but Nina, who had volunteered to help out so that she could keep an eye on Gretchen after the unfortunate tarot reading, seemed determined to horn in on Gretchen's directorial turf. Nina apparently didn't understand the role of assistant director.

Gretchen fervently wished that she'd never mentioned the high school stage production she'd had a minor role in years ago. Suddenly she was the director of *Ding Dong Dead,* the certified expert on play production. Certifiable, was more like it. She had to be nuts to have agreed to take this on. The title of director didn't suit her, as she was quickly finding out. She didn't have the necessary air of authority. But Nina didn't have the people skills, judging by the pleading expressions on the cast's faces.

"A few more minutes before we start up again would be appreciated," Julie agreed.

They looked expectantly toward Gretchen, waiting to see if she'd challenge Nina's bid for power. She really should say something that would reestablish her status as commander of this listing ship. But after last night's trip to the cemetery, Gretchen hadn't slept well. Nightmares weren't anything new, but her usual dreams had morphed into something different — monsters she couldn't see, screams she couldn't scream, cliffs, falling, and a dead woman's sightless stare.

Gretchen managed a nod to indicate her agreement with the cast.

Nina rolled her eyes.

Bonnie, who played the role of Craig Bitters in the production, flipped off the cheap male wig, exposing a tight wig cap underneath. Beneath the cap, crushed against her scalp, was Bonnie's own red wig, which she wore every day to conceal the large bald spot on her crown.

"I'm proud of our stage setting," Gretchen said to distract them from further dissent. The play, which had been written by her mother, Caroline, took place inside a doll collector's home, in a room devoted entirely to Barbie dolls and teddy bears. They had found a damaged pink Barbie house and had converted it into display cases, filling it with dolls and bears. The six-foot Barbie had been donated by one of the club members. The overall effect was perfect. At times, Gretchen could suspend belief and actually imagine that she was in one of the club member's homes.

"When that gun went off, I almost peed

in my pants," Bonnie said.

Julie giggled. Cast as Craig's long-suffering wife, Doris, Julie came to rehearsal each day dressed for her part. Although Gretchen had insisted that she was perfect already, Julie had dyed her brown hair black and styled it in a messy updo. Heavy makeup and a red cotton sweater with embroidered teddy bears completed the package.

Gretchen felt the tension break as the group of doll collectors took turns stepping down from the stage of the banquet hall, all talking at once. She watched them head for the break area in the next room.

Gretchen went over the play notes her mother had left for her. Without them, she'd be lost. Her spirit brightened as she read. The play was a modern farce with great lines for all the characters. Doris, played by Julie, would accidentally shoot her husband, and the women of the doll club would form a conspiratorial bond in a humorous attempt to cover up the murder.

After working with Bonnie in Craig's role, Gretchen felt that the end for her, or rather for him, couldn't come soon enough.

"Oh, no!" Nina rushed toward the stage, where her pampered schnoodle Tutu chomped down on a prop, one of Bonnie's

beloved teddy bears, which she had reluctantly contributed to the stage setting after
extracting a solemn promise from all the
members that her treasures would return to
her private collection without so much as a
smudge or wrinkle.

*Not a chance of fulfilling that promise with
Her Highness running wild.*

Tutu leapt off the stage with the bear
firmly planted between her canine incisors
and circled the large banquet room with
Nina in hot pursuit. She finally trapped the
pooch in a corner and coaxed her into
releasing the stuffed animal.

"Tutu just demonstrated one of the main
reasons why we decided to ban pets from
rehearsals," Gretchen reminded her aunt.

"I wasn't part of that decision," Nina said,
wiping Bonnie's teddy bear on the hem of
her red and white polka-dot sundress. Tutu,
always accessorized to complement Nina's
flamboyant attire, had large red and white
bows attached to each ear.

"You aren't a voting member of the club,"
Gretchen said. "If you'd ante up and pay
your dues like the rest of us, you'd have
more say."

Aunt Nina didn't "do" dolls, but her
unique personality had made her a welcome
addition to the club. That was, until recently

when her tyrannical behavior indicated that she was on borrowed club time.

Aside from her New Age endeavors, Nina owned a specialty business that catered to those club members who had furry little pets. She'd talked many of them into adopting what she called purse dogs, three- to five-pound miniature dogs. Then she offered training courses to teach the little things to stay put inside their travel purses — and to hide whenever their owners entered no-pet zones like restaurants or supermarkets.

Nina had succeeded in her mission to place pups with as many club members as possible, and she *was* very good at training them — both the canines and their humans. What she hadn't done well was train her own dog, Tutu, a miniature diva she had rescued from the animal control center when no one came forward to claim her. Tutu was self-absorbed and completely unteachable. Gretchen didn't know what Nina saw in the critter.

Nina had even convinced Gretchen herself to adopt Nimrod, a curly coated black teacup poodle.

"Nimrod's at doggie day care," Gretchen said, reflecting on her tiny companion, always surprised at how much she missed him when he wasn't at her side. "That's where Tutu should be right now."

The schnoodle stared at Gretchen as though she understood English perfectly. They were at war, the beady eyes told her, and Tutu planned on winning every battle.

"We have important issues to discuss," Nina said, waving a ring-studded hand. "The luncheon is coming up fast, only two weeks away and so much to do. We still have to meet with the caterer, pick up table arrangements, prepare the silent auction, and whip this bunch into shape. The entire event is turning into a disaster."

"It'll be fine." Gretchen sat down on the edge of the stage, not believing her own words. They hadn't anticipated the amount of work involved in presenting a play with a cast completely devoid of talent or any innate ability to follow simple directions or remember lines. "Everything will come together."

And all the time away from the repair shop had Gretchen worried. She loved the partnership with her mother, the finely tuned team they had become. But dolls in need of attention were piling up daily, especially now that they finally had access to the marvelous Spanish Colonial Revival with its complex blend of Mexican and Spanish influences. The house was structurally sound, but needed a thorough cleaning after years of standing empty. And cataloging and organizing the displays would take more time than they originally had thought. Her mother had been working long hours at the new museum for the last few days. No one was in the workshop.

Two weeks and life will return to normal, she reminded herself.

"We have several hundred guests registered for the luncheon and the theater presentation." Nina sat down beside her. "And more ticket requests coming in every day."

"Good work. Our dream is coming true."

Nina gave her a doubtful look. "At first I thought it was wonderful that the club had been offered the opportunity to renovate the house and open it as a doll museum, but my radar is telling me that something is wrong. Your last tarot reading isn't reassuring me either."

The cast began wandering back into the banquet hall dressed in their street clothes, their purses slung over their shoulders. "We had a meeting in the break room," Bonnie said. "We're on strike."

"I didn't get a vote," Nina said.

"You're the reason we're striking," Bonnie

said to Nina.

"It's been stressful," Julie said, lagging behind the rebellion. "We've been working hard. Let's take the rest of the day off to rejuvenate and try again tomorrow."

The other members of the play didn't look as though they agreed with Julie.

As the cast filed out, all Gretchen could do was hope they'd come back.

Nina came out of the break room with two cups of coffee. "After what you went through last night, you should be the one taking the day off. How awful for that poor woman."

They sat down in upholstered chairs on the stage.

"Right now I'm extremely worried about Nacho and Daisy," Gretchen said. "Why didn't Daisy signal to me when I was at the cemetery?"

"How did they ever manage before they met you?"

The two homeless people had been a source of frustration for Gretchen ever since she'd met and become friends with them, shortly after her move to Arizona. She wanted to help them, but she assumed that meant they had to change. She was learning fast that her method wasn't working.

Still, she didn't want to give up.

"I called the police station without finding out anything. Daisy isn't answering her cell. I don't want to bother Matt until later. I'm sure he worked through the night."

"Nacho and Daisy will be fine. It's this project and your safety that I'm worried about. Everything's off-kilter. Auras are wrong. Everything."

Her aunt was unlike most people, but her views weren't without merit. She saw life through a different colored lens, and though she didn't like to admit it, Gretchen understood much of Nina's madness.

"If I'd had a vote," her aunt continued, "I would have voted no to taking this on."

"Why?" For someone on the opposing side, Nina had certainly waded in to take over control of the play.

"We don't know anything about the owner. Caroline went down and looked at the deed. It's titled to something called The Smart Investment Trust. That doesn't tell us anything."

The arrangement was unusual, but also a good deal for the club. According to the terms of the agreement with the house's owner, the club would have several fundraisers to help with refurbishing and operating costs, and they would convert the home into a museum. In return, the owner would allow them to remodel as they wished and then use any revenues generated to keep the museum open and running.

Nina scowled. "That wormy little attorney who is representing the owner, what's his name?"

"Dean McNalty."

"Him. There's not one good reason why he can't tell us who owns the house. I'd like to get answers out of him even if it means wringing his scrawny little neck."

"Such violence from a proclaimed pacifist."

"I'm feeling a bit stressed," Nina admitted.

"Not only do we have a beautiful old building to work with, but the original owners were also avid collectors. The house is filled with boxes of dolls."

With what they'd already found inside the house and with the dolls the members had eagerly offered to donate, they might have opened the first floor to visitors by the end of the month. If only the paperwork hadn't taken so long. She and her mother had received keys and had taken their first walk-through only three days ago.

Gretchen sipped her coffee and looked around the empty room. "There isn't anything more we can do here. Let me show you the museum. We have our work cut out for us, but the possibilities are limitless."

6

There are many ways to place dolls for display. They can be arranged by size, by type, or by color. A grouping of dolls dressed all in white can be very dramatic. Or you can place dolls in scenes, paying close attention to appropriate furnishings for your doll's particular era.

Preservation of your dolls is the key to their longevity. Keep them away from direct sunlight and florescent lights. Room temperature should be between sixty-five degrees and seventy degrees. Closed cases are preferable to open where the dolls would be exposed to dirt, dust, and insects.

— From *World of Dolls* by Caroline Birch

Gretchen and Nina walked the three short blocks from the rehearsal hall to the museum, led by Tutu. Caroline came out of the house while they were standing on the sidewalk admiring the architecture. Gretchen loved the Spanish Colonial Revival. It had a low-pitched red-tile roof, arched windows, and an asymmetrical design that Gretchen found intriguing. And it was right in the heart of one of the few remaining historic districts in the downtown area.

To complete the perfect picture, a small balcony overlooked the street, and behind the house stood a tiny caretaker's cottage. *La casita* in Spanish.

"The house is owned by an eccentric, hermitlike woman, according to the owner's attorney," Caroline said, standing next to them. "No one has lived here for many years."

The entire doll club had been present for the inspection so Gretchen already knew that the home had been neglected for a very long time. At least most of the dolls had been boxed up and stored away from the damaging effects of dust and sunlight. And what a massive collection it was turning out to be! Generations of this family's members must have been avid collectors.

"Come in and see the progress we've made," Caroline said.

"Just so you know," Nina said, "I'm firmly against what you are doing."

"Oh, really?" Caroline said. "Then you

should go shopping. Come on, Gretchen."

The last thing her aunt could stand was being excluded. "I'll stay," she said. "Someone has to protect you two from your own actions."

Gretchen paused on the sidewalk to admire a large sign, finding herself once again in awe of her mother's ability to negotiate. World of Dolls Museum, the sign read. A smaller sign hung beneath it announcing that it would open soon. "I like it. You convinced the new owner to name the museum after your doll book. A smart move."

Caroline beamed. "I had to work through the attorney," she said. "He had to carry the request and subsequent questions and answers back and forth."

"Any luck getting the name of our generous benefactor while you were being so clever?"

"None. We'll have to tie the attorney down and torture it out of him."

Gretchen couldn't imagine a worse idea than being trapped with the little man who had approached them with the offer. She'd be the one under torture. "Let's see what's happening inside," she said, opening the museum door and stepping into the World of Dolls.

No one was working in the front of the museum, but Gretchen could hear singing coming from the back of the house.

Caroline set her purse on a counter. "April and I have been working nonstop the last two days. What you see here is all we've managed to organize so far."

"I love it already," Gretchen said.

Fabulous displays began at the entryway. The minute she entered Gretchen felt as though she were on an exciting Disney ride. Smiling dolls with colorful clothing were placed in settings that would draw visitors farther into the museum. The displays were like scrumptious appetizers, a promise to the diner that every course would be as flavorful as the first.

"I have a few calls to make," Caroline said. "Look around. You have such a good eye for design, Nina. Come back in, oh, about fifteen minutes and tell me what you think would be the best layout."

Gretchen and Nina followed the melody down the hall and into a room on the left where fellow club member and good friend, April, was humming away while she arranged dolls. She had a rich, well-projected voice.

April was the doll club's appraiser. She had a keen eye for detail and a natural talent that Gretchen envied. April could touch a piece of doll clothing and tell you exactly where it came from and when. She was also Gretchen's best friend along with Nina. April was about Gretchen's own age but looked older than Nina (who, at twelve years younger than Caroline, was almost closer to Gretchen's age than her own sister's). April was a big-boned woman who wore muumuus and colored socks with her sandals, and she absolutely adored a tiny Chihuahua named Enrico, another of Nina's successful adoption placements.

Gretchen and her aunt stood in the doorway and listened to the melody until April noticed them.

"Hey, what are you doing here? Aren't you supposed to be directing?" she asked.

"We gave the cast the day off," Nina said as if it had been her idea.

"Oh good. Julie offered to help us after rehearsal," April said. "That means she might come early."

"Look at this!" Gretchen exclaimed, stunned by the wonderful collectibles spread out on a metal worktable. "Wow!"

"I'm going to do a walk-through," Nina said. "My expertise is needed elsewhere."

"Go and create," April said.

April was thrilled to show Gretchen the

display she was working on. She had almost completed a collection of Robert Tonner dolls — sixteen-inch Tyler Wentworth dolls with their ultramodern hair fashions and up-to-date casual wear. Fleece, peasant tops, jean jackets, accessories. Gretchen also admired a collection of Seventeen dolls by Ashton-Drake, wearing hip teenage fashions.

"But some of these are new dolls," Gretchen said, dazzled but puzzled. "They aren't old enough to be part of the original collection, are they?"

April smiled. "One of the ladies who is coming to our luncheon donated them after I solicited for a contribution. Can you believe it?"

Gretchen shook her head in wonder, feeling very emotional. The doll collectors of Phoenix were some of the most generous, loving people she had ever met. This collection went far beyond her wildest expectations. If this, Gretchen's first room of dolls, could make her tear up, what else was in store for her?

"I've been so busy trying to shape the play and the players that I forgot about our actual cause, this museum." Gretchen wiped away a tear of joy.

"And this is only the beginning." April

stood back from the display with a critical eye. "Wait until after the fundraiser, when we have more money. Eventually we'll open the upstairs rooms, too." She picked up one of the dolls from the table and smoothed the hair. "This is one of the original owner's dolls. Remember Starr?"

How could Gretchen forget the teenager dolls? "And Starr's friends, Tracy and Kelley," she said.

April held up two more 1980s dolls. "We don't have a Shaun doll, but I'm on the lookout. He's my favorite. He was the guy everybody wanted to date."

"He's a doll, April," Gretchen said, laughing. "Not a real guy."

"Not like your hunk," April said. "If Matt were a doll, he'd be Shaun. Hot, sexy, smart, fun."

"He *is* all that."

"Starr and her doll friends went to Springfield High," April said. "They came with schoolbooks, tambourines for their band, yearbooks, and all the latest fashions from the eighties."

"Those were the days," Gretchen said. "Roller-skating, pep rallies, wholesome fun."

April snorted. "Wholesome fun! We watched all those teenage slaughter movies. Remember those? Remember *Friday the 13th* with Adrienne King and Kevin Bacon? What a hunk that Kevin was. We'd be glued to the screen, chomping on popcorn, watching those poor camp counselor kids get chased around and killed by a psychopath." She snorted again. "I wouldn't exactly call it a wholesome time, but it sure was fun."

"Where's Enrico?" Gretchen asked.

April motioned to a Mexican tapestry purse hanging on the back of a chair. "Sleeping."

"What are you —"

Gretchen's next question was interrupted by a glass-shattering scream coming from above, someplace on the second floor of the massive house.

She knew that voice.

"Nina!" she shouted, rushing down the hall.

Another scream.

She reached the circular staircase and ran up them, taking them two at a time.

Nina screamed for the third time.

7

Gretchen reached the top of the stairs with her mother right behind her. They stopped at the landing and listened. Caroline, her breath ragged, grasped the dark wood banister on the landing for support.

"Are you okay?" Gretchen asked her mother, worried.

Caroline nodded. "I'll be all right. Where do you think she is? Nina!"

There was no response.

"You go that way," Gretchen said, pointing to a hall on the left before turning to the one to the right.

She listened to her mother's footsteps on the tile floor, then heard her open a door and call out her sister's name.

Gretchen did the same. As she approached the second room, she heard a tiny, muffled voice. "I'm in here."

Gretchen followed Nina's voice into a room that had been converted into a large storage closet. Every bit of space was filled with boxes of dolls that hadn't been catalogued yet. Stacks and stacks of them with little room to enter.

"Where are you?"

"Here."

"I found her," Gretchen called loud enough for her mother to hear. Then she squeezed down a narrow aisle between the boxes until she found her aunt on the floor.

Nina was a sight to behold. All that was visible were two red high heels and bare calves sticking out from underneath a display case piled high with boxes. "Help," Nina croaked, her voice muffled under the case.

"What are you doing down there?" Wasn't this exactly in character for her aunt? Nina wasn't happy unless she was the center of attention. What better way than to worm under a piece of furniture and start screaming.

Her aunt wiggled her legs, almost stabbing Gretchen with a spiky heel.

Caroline appeared in the doorway and accurately read Gretchen's annoyed expression.

"Nina's physically okay," her mother called down the steps to April. "It's her mental state we're concerned with." She squeezed into the room. "What was all the screaming about?"

"I'm stuck," Nina cried. "Help me get out."

Gretchen lifted and moved several boxes, stacking piles even higher to make more room to work. Nina's heels continued to swing wildly. "Quit kicking or we'll leave you to get out by yourself." Her aunt lowered her feet.

Gretchen cleared enough space to get on one side of the case while Caroline got on the other. They tipped it back to release a discombobulated Nina. She was a mess. Mascara was smudged under her eyes, and her hair stood straight up, smashed into a Mohawk.

"How did you get under there in the first place?" Caroline said, holding on to her sister's arm to steady her as she rose. "Why would you crawl under a display case? Look at your dress. It's filthy."

Nina acted like she didn't hear them, focusing instead on the floor. "Tutu, darling, come to momma. Baby dolly, pooh bear, come, come."

Whimpering came from behind another stack of boxes. Nina edged through and extracted the schnoodle, giving her a big bear hug. "I was so worried."

"What is going on?" Caroline said. "You screamed like you were about to be murdered."

"It was terrible," Nina said, her lip quivering. "But it's gone now."

"What's gone?" Gretchen scanned the room for poisonous critters. A black widow spider would have her leaping from the room, leaving the rest to fend for themselves.

Her aunt didn't even hear her.

"Give me Tutu," Caroline said, "before you drop her. And pull yourself together. You frightened us badly."

"Give me a minute."

While Caroline attempted to get an answer from Nina, Gretchen wandered the narrow pathways. A small wooden container about the size of a shoe box was propped open on top of one of the stacks.

"That's it," Nina said, pointing at the little box with a trembling finger. "It came out of there."

Gretchen edged away. "What? A spider?"

"No," Nina said. "Nothing like that."

Cautiously, Gretchen made her way over and picked up the wooden container. "What a beautiful doll trunk!" Old-fashioned travel stickers were pasted on the trunk in random fashion. Flowered paper lined the inside of

59

the trunk, and it had a tiny drawer on one side where accessories could be stored. "It's old but in very good shape," Gretchen said, bringing it back with her.

"It's also empty," Caroline noted, glaring at her sister before saying to Gretchen, "Travelers used to apply stickers to their travel trunks. These are faded with age, and they are certainly authentic. Even the hinges are antiques. A lucky doll must have toured the world inside of it."

"This one is from Cairo." Gretchen had to squint to make out the lettering on the worn stickers. "Another from London."

She glanced at her aunt. Nina was pale and leaned against the display case. "What came out of the trunk?" she said to her. "A bat?"

"No, not even close." She patted her hair down with both hands and eyed the trunk suspiciously. "You're going to laugh at me."

"No we won't," Gretchen said.

"Yes, you will."

Caroline crossed her arms and scowled. Gretchen closed the trunk lid and waited.

"I came up here to look around like you asked me to, Caroline, to give you design ideas. The trunk was right over there where you found it, Gretchen, but it was closed. When I came in the room, I thought something inside of it called out to me."

"Like what?" Gretchen asked. "Like, 'Nina, oh, Nina'?"

"You're laughing."

"No, I'm not. I believe you."

One time, when Gretchen had ignored her aunt's warnings, brushing them off as fanciful imaginings, Nina had almost been killed trying to prove herself.

Gretchen would never laugh at her aunt's antics again. If nothing else, Nina added a little more spice to the already flavorful southwestern atmosphere. This, though, was the first time inanimate objects had spoken to her.

"Okay then." Nina finished arranging her wayward hair into a semblance of her bob, jeweled fingers fluttering. "I heard something like an 'ooooohhh' coming from the area around the trunk. As I went closer, I discovered that the sound was coming from inside it. The sound was like someone moaning or like the wind howling."

Gretchen and Caroline exchanged glances.

"I opened the trunk. What a mistake." She sighed heavily and let her breath rasp out. "Then," she said, animated now, the actress in her coming to the surface, "a ghost flew out of it, right into my face and through my body like I didn't exist. It was like a billow of smoke. For a second I thought I was a goner. But here I am."

Gretchen gaped.

"I don't know what to say," Caroline said slowly.

Loud sputtering laughter came from behind them.

April stood in the doorway. "Ha, ha, ho, ho, hee, hee."

Gretchen was about to lose control, too. "April," she warned, holding back her own belly laugh, "you have to stop."

"Hee-hee, haw-haw. I know, I know. I'm trying." April pulled a tissue from a pocket and blew her nose. "What if you released a genie?" she said, cracking up again. "Wouldn't that be sweet? We better find it and get our three wishes. Oh, this is rich."

"It frightened me almost to death," Nina said, offended. "Even Tutu saw it. She ducked behind some boxes, and I dove for the floor and crawled under the display case as fast as I could. That's when I got stuck."

That set April off again.

Caroline attempted to hide a smile, but it finally got the best of her and she let loose and joined April.

"This isn't funny," Nina said.

"All I can see in my mind is you stuck under the case," April screeched.

"I'm so happy I was able to entertain you," Nina snapped. "But something real flew out of that doll trunk, and I'm going to find out what it was."

"Nina," Caroline said, attempting to get serious, "we have enough to do without chasing after ghosts. Quit trying to make life more complicated than it already is. Let's get the luncheon over with and the museum ready for the opening. Then you can chase ghosts."

"I'm not sure that's the best advice." Gretchen wasn't about to let this opportunity get away. What a great way to keep Nina busy and away from the play production. "We'll be spending a lot of time at the museum, and we wouldn't want to share space with a malicious spirit, would we? I think it's important that Nina pursue this."

"I plan to." Nina was back in form. "Ghosts are real," she said. "I just overreacted to its appearance because I wasn't prepared. I'm going to the New Age shop for more information."

"Good idea," Gretchen said.

"But I already know a little something about the subject of ghosts," Nina continued. "We need to be alert for strange sounds or weird smells."

"Lights going on and off," Gretchen added.

"Blasts of cold air." Nina had a glint in her eyes. This was her kind of problem. "Objects moving. Someone has unfinished business on earth, and I'm going to find out what it is."

8

Caroline steps from the car. Matt Albright waits in front of the police station to escort her inside. He has impeccable manners — opening doors for her, offering coffee, performing the obligatory small talk. *How have you been? How's Nina? By the way, you have a beautiful daughter with a matching soul.*

He scores extra points for mentioning Gretchen's inner beauty.

Caroline is sure he feels the same as she does under the circumstances, uncomfortable because of their personal relationship, wanting to get the unpleasant task over with as quickly as possible.

The mother and the boyfriend size each other up.

"After you," he says, showing her into a room.

She doesn't really want to know the truth, so why did she make the call to the detective? Out of a sense of truth and justice? Yes. But also out of fear.

He leaves her alone. A large mirror on the wall shows her that her face is as pale as her silver hair. Is it a two-way mirror? Is someone on the other side?

She sits down at a square table in the middle of the room and rakes her silver hair with her fingers, thinking of her daughter. Two nuts from the same black walnut tree, her husband used to say when he was alive. Before the fatal car accident that took him but thankfully left her daughter physically unharmed. She hopes the emotional scars have faded if not totally healed. Gretchen assures her they have, but her daughter's nightmares tell Caroline the truth.

God, she misses him. Nothing could ever make up for her loss. Nobody, anywhere, could replace that man. Gretchen reminds her so much of him, although everyone else says mother and daughter resemble each other. They have the same strong build, but her daughter has her father's inquisitive mind, boldly taking on and dealing with life's hardships, sometimes acting a little too impulsively for her own good.

Matt comes back into the room with two cups of coffee. He's nothing at all like his chatty mother, Bonnie. He's secretive and cautious.

The detective sits across from her at the scarred table in the shabby room with tired furniture and bad lighting. A manila file folder lies between them.

"How did she die?" Caroline asks, the word tumbling out beyond her control.

Matt doesn't answer her question. "You don't have to do this, you know?" he says, but she can tell that he's eager for anything that might assist him in his search.

They have the same strong sense of justice.

"What if I'm right?" she says. "You need to know as quickly as possible to catch whoever did this."

"What if you're wrong? Either way, it isn't necessary that you be the one to identify her. Give me a name and I'll track down the family. It will be easy to find out if it's the woman you think it is. Just give me a name."

Caroline shakes her head. "I don't want to be responsible for an incorrect identification. I don't want to intrude on the wrong family's life. Please, it's important to me to make sure." She glances up at the mirror. "I've never done this before, identified someone."

"It takes some getting used to."

"Will we go into the morgue?"

Matt grins, but not with his eyes. "No. I have pictures."

She wants to take a sip of her coffee from the foam cup he has placed in front of her, but she knows that her hand will shake. That's the tip-off. She might look calm on the outside, but the way she handles a coffee cup will reveal the opposite. Hers would slosh back and forth. She'd spill it.

"I need to know how she died," Caroline says again, her eyes flicking to a file lying on the table between them, wondering why the cause of death is so important to her.

After all, dead is dead.

"Blows to the back of the head," Matt says. "With a blunt instrument."

Visions of a raised hammer, a clenched fist, the descent.

Why did I even ask?

He opens the file, withdraws what is obviously a stack of photographs, holds them so she can see only the back side, like a folded hand of cards in a poker game.

"I'd like to see the doll again," Caroline says, stalling for time. She sees Matt shudder and says quickly, "A picture, I meant. You must have one."

Not much gets through this tough detective's steely coat of manly armor, but Caroline knows Matt's embarrassing secret: he suffers from a condition known as pedio-phobia. In layman's terms, he is afraid of dolls. Caroline has witnessed the panic attacks, seen him work up an unnatural sweat, watched him struggle to breathe normally whenever he came into viewing range of any kind of doll.

He sorts through the file and hands a photo to her.

Caroline stares at the fairy doll, even more sure of her suspicions.

Matt busies himself by placing another picture on the table, facedown. Selects another. He returns the others to the file folder and picks up the remaining ones. "Ready?" he says.

Caroline doesn't answer immediately.

Then she nods.

9

"A ghost?" Bonnie said, sitting on the edge of the stage and fussing with her handlebar mustache. "What that woman won't think of next."

"She's off to the historical society to go through records," Gretchen said. "She's hoping something will turn up in the history of the house to explain its ghostly activity."

April, surrounded by yards of billowing pink material, paused in the act of threading a needle. She glanced over the top of her reading glasses. "She wants all of us to stay away from the museum."

"That's not going to happen." Gretchen watched the amateur seamstress sew a ball gown for the six-foot Barbie mannequin. April spent more time ripping out and redoing than moving forward.

"Hope Nina's close encounter doesn't come back to 'haunt' us," April said, giggling.

Bonnie put on the man's wig over her own red one. "Nina should hire a ghost hunter to track it down and eliminate it," she said.

Gretchen's cell phone rang.

Finally!

"I'm out of jail," Daisy said from the other end of the line. "They got around to questioning me early this morning. I'm free, but I need a place to stay tonight. They won't release my things to me yet."

The homeless woman could live without shelter, but take her shopping cart filled with junk and she didn't know what to do.

"Of course, you're always welcome at our house." More than she knew. One of these days, Gretchen hoped to permanently convert the homeless woman. So far, though, Daisy hadn't stayed more than a night or two. Then she'd vanished, only to reappear back on the street. Maybe this would be the time she stayed and turned her life around. "Where's Nacho?" Gretchen asked.

"I haven't seen him or any of the other men yet, but he'll come around sooner or later. I'm not worried about him." Daisy, usually in a delusional state, sounded amazingly lucid.

"What happened in the cemetery, Daisy?"

"We don't get involved. You know that. All

71

I can say is that we'd have been long gone if we suspected that kind of trouble."

"You didn't see anything? Hear anything?"

"I don't get involved," the homeless woman insisted. "Catch you later."

And Daisy disconnected.

"Five minutes," Gretchen called out to the cast. "And we'll take it from the top."

"Get the pistol," she heard Bonnie say. "We're going to do us some shooting."

Gretchen worked with the cast all afternoon, going over the second act, the act when Doris was about to find out that all the women in the room had dallied with her husband. Bonnie flubbed one line after another. Julie ran interference, displaying a level of peacekeeping skills that Gretchen wished she had.

In the corner of the room, April busied herself with her sewing project. The rat-a-tat of the sewing machine caused a brief flare-up among the doll club members that was extinguished when April agreed to wait until rehearsal was over to run it again. Instead, she fitted her creation on the enormous doll, sticking pins here and there. Gretchen noticed that one sleeve was much shorter than the other.

Halfway through the second act, Gretchen remembered an important detail. "When is

Karen coming to work on the lighting? Isn't she the one who offered?"

"She *was* going to do it," April said through a mouthful of pins, "but she's babysitting for her granddaughter the weekend of the performance. She can't help."

"When were you going to tell me?"

"I forgot."

"Can you work them?" Gretchen didn't have much choice. She'd take anybody she could get.

"I'm way too busy with the museum and my sewing project."

"But you have to."

"I don't know anything about lights, and I refuse to be bullied into it."

From the look on April's face, she wasn't going to budge from her position behind the sewing machine.

One more thing for Gretchen to take care of.

The afternoon went quickly, not exactly without hitches, but at least Julie fired the murder weapon at the right moment and Bonnie's mustache stayed attached to her face when she hit the floor. It was a statement about the cast that Gretchen was thankful for such small things. At four o'clock Nina hustled in, led by Tutu, who pranced along on her pink leash.

"Find out anything about the ghost?" Gretchen asked.

"I'm pointed in the right direction. Where is he?"

"Uh . . . where's who?"

"Brandon's picking me up here. I absolutely love that man, hair the color of wheat and green brooding eyes that speak of depth and danger."

"Oh, brother," April said.

Nina had been casually dating a Scottsdale detective, Brandon Kline, who was a good friend of Matt's. Brandon and Nina were made from the same cloth. He encouraged her when she went off on one of her New Age tangents.

"I haven't seen him," Gretchen said.

"I'll help you direct until he arrives." Nina swept toward the stage. The cast members saw her charging and were more nimble than usual in their race for the break room.

Gretchen had to think of a distraction quickly to keep Nina busy until her man arrived. "What's the story with the ghost? You didn't tell me what you found out."

April tee-heed.

"Are you smirking?" Nina confronted April.

"Nope," said April, bending over the sewing machine, making it roar to life.

Nina took a seat in Gretchen's director's chair. "I found a picture of the family that lived in the house in the early 1920s. Spanish Colonial Revival architecture dates back to around that time, so the family must have built the home. The owner's name was John Swilling, and, get this, he had a daughter."

April stopped the machine. "Well, that's it then," she said. "Either John or his daughter is the ghost."

Gretchen couldn't tell whether April was seriously considering the problem or subtly mocking the idea. Nina suspected hidden sarcasm and scowled at her.

"Go on," Gretchen said.

"Flora was the girl's name," Nina continued. "I found a sepia photograph of her. Flora must have been about ten years old at the time the picture was taken — it shows her holding a doll in her arms. And there's more."

"Do tell," April said.

Another scowl before Nina addressed Gretchen, completely ignoring April. "That doll's travel trunk is in the picture. I could even see some of the travel stickers."

She waited for a response.

"Is that important?" Gretchen asked, suspecting full well that it was. She couldn't put her finger on the reason, but something about the trunk intrigued her. She'd like to get another look at it.

"Don't you see?" Nina said, impatient with her. "Flora Swilling is our ghost! Something happened to her inside the house, and I'm going to find out what it was. And I suspect that it's equally crucial to locate the doll she's holding in the photograph."

"Why would we have to find the doll?"

"Flora could be haunting the house because she can't find it. Once the doll is reunited with the travel trunk, she might be able to rest in peace."

"The doll will rest in peace?" April asked.

"No! Flora."

"What does the doll look like?" Gretchen asked.

Nina slapped her head. "I forgot the copy of the picture. I stopped home and changed purses. I left it in the other one."

Gretchen mentally pictured the pile of repair work and play notes on her desk and wished she could help with the ghost hunting or arrange displays at the museum instead. She had been coerced into taking the most detailed and frustrating job. "Nina," she said, "I don't have time to help you with your search. In a few weeks, after the show, I'll be available, if you can wait that long. Right now I have to focus on the rehearsals."

"And you should." Nina gave her a look of compassion. "I'm going to take some of that responsibility so you don't have to take it on alone. You're absolutely right; the ghost has been haunting the house for over one hundred years. A few more weeks won't matter."

Oh, no. Nina was back. "I didn't mean *you* should stop," Gretchen stammered, trying to rectify her mistake. "Bonnie thinks you should hire a ghost buster, and I agree completely."

"Really? She thinks that, does she?" Nina raised an eyebrow and straightened her shoulders. "If Bonnie and the rest of the cast would ever get done with their snack break, I'd tell her that I'm going to make a great ghost hunter. This job," she said, "I can handle myself."

With a great show of dignity, Nina sauntered toward the doorway to meet her date.

Nina, Gretchen thought with a sense of accomplishment, *will be gone for the duration of the rehearsals.*

10

"Where were you all day?" Gretchen asked her mother from a lounge chair near the pool. After spending hours on her feet, it felt good to get off them. She appreciated all the months of the year they could sit outside as they were now. Arizona living had its advantages. Nimrod slept on her lap after a busy day of socializing at doggy day care.

Caroline sat down beside her. "I ran errands and dropped off completed projects. The business still needs some attention, if we don't want to lose customers. Work is piling up. I'll be glad when this project is over, and we can get back to our usual routine."

Her mother looked tired, pale, and anxious. With everything she had going — her work as an author, touring and promotion, the doll repair business, and now the museum restoration — no wonder she looked exhausted.

Wobbles purred next to Gretchen while staring intensely at the sleeping Nimrod, always on the alert for unwanted attention. He never let down his guard. The teacup poodle loved Wobbles, but the sentiment wasn't returned, although Wobbles did tolerate the energetic puppy. Tutu was another story altogether. Wobbles and Tutu defined the phrase *fighting like cats and dogs.*

"Daisy's staying with us tonight," Gretchen said. "She's freshening up in the spare bedroom."

"Wonderful. I've missed her company."

"She said she has important news but wanted to wait until we were both together before announcing it. Something special, she says, and she's very excited."

"My ears were ringing." Daisy came outside, all radiant and scrubbed, wearing a terry robe from the closet. Gretchen had gone out of her way to stock the spare room with luxuries to lure their occasional guest. "Hey, doggie." She scooped up Nimrod.

The homeless woman had an affinity with animals. Even Tutu loved her.

"Sit down and tell us your news," Caroline said.

"First tell me about the museum. How is it coming along? When will it open?"

"We've only begun," Caroline said. "But

I'm thrilled with the results so far."

"I wish I could say the same about the fundraiser," Gretchen added. "Today I learned that we don't have anyone to handle lights. But I'll figure out something." She patted the seat of the lounge chair next to her. "Sit down and tell all."

"I can't sit. I want to bounce right off the stars." Daisy whirled, robe twirling. "Nacho proposed!" she said. "We're getting married."

Gretchen and Caroline yelped with pleasure. Daisy blushed. Her middle-aged face took on a young girl's glow.

"I'll have to put my acting career on hold," she said. "But it will only be temporary."

"Sure. You can always go back to acting later," Gretchen agreed.

One of Daisy's consuming delusions was her belief that Hollywood scouts would discover her on the crowded streets of Phoenix and she would become an Oscar-winning actress. It hadn't happened so far, but Daisy remained optimistic.

Today, the bride-to-be was more grounded than usual.

"When and where is this extraordinary event taking place?" Caroline asked.

"At the courthouse on the first of June.

We don't want a lengthy engagement, but we need to give our out-of-town friends time to arrive. Everyone we know is invited."

Gretchen could picture an entire homeless community descending en masse to converge on the Phoenix courthouse.

They'd never make it through security.

And where would the couple honeymoon? In Eternal View Cemetery? Would they dine at the rescue mission? She couldn't completely wrap her mind around their future together, but they'd coexisted until now in perfect contentment.

Caroline winked at Gretchen. She nodded back, knowing what was coming.

"Why don't we have the wedding right here?" Caroline said. "We could find someone to perform the ceremony on the patio and have a reception afterward. And everyone would still be invited." She grabbed Daisy's hand. "Please say yes."

Daisy radiated happiness. "I'd love that!" she said. "I have to go call my friends and tell them about the change in plans."

And off she went, bouncing on a dreamy cloud with the teacup poodle in her arms. "Daisy is a mystery," Gretchen said. "Where did she get the cell phone? And who is maintaining the service for her?"

"Who knows? I think she came from a

good home life. She's kind and generous and has impeccable manners when it suits her."

"I wish she'd agree to accept psychological help and get off the street."

"It's her choice. She's the only one who can make a change happen. All we can do is support her decision and help in small ways. Besides, she *is* working on improving herself. She's trying a new medication."

"Really!" No wonder Daisy seemed so rational lately. "The pills are working."

"She told me about her doctor's visit last week, but I wasn't supposed to tell you."

"Why not?"

"You tend to get too involved."

"Marriage will be good for both of them. Now if only —" Gretchen was about to voice her concerns about Nacho and his battle with alcoholism when her mother interrupted.

"All we can do is support them," Caroline reminded her. "When is Matt picking you up?"

"He's bringing dinner in an hour, enough for all of us." She glanced up at Camelback Mountain, appreciating the view from the patio as much today as the day she'd moved into her mother's cabana. "Then we're hitting the mountain ridges."

"The quest for another bird?"

Gretchen nodded. *Something like that.*

"Listen, we have to have a conversation before Matt arrives."

"Sure, what's up?" Her mother looked too serious. *Please don't tell me your cancer is back.* That particular fear hung on the edge of Gretchen's mind all the time.

"Don't look at me that way," Caroline said. "I'm perfectly fine. It's about the woman in the cemetery."

"What about her?" Gretchen had kept the dead woman at the back of her thoughts most of the day. Staying busy had helped.

"The fantasy doll looked vaguely familiar to me. I thought about it all night, and this morning I knew for sure I was right. It was so long ago, I didn't believe it could be possible. But unfortunately, it was." Caroline reached for her glass on the table — her favorite cocktail, a single-malt scotch, ice, no water. "I know who the murder victim is."

"What?" exclaimed Gretchen.

"I met Matt at the police station. He showed me photographs and I identified her. She was older than I'd pictured her. It's strange, when you haven't seen someone for a long time, you expect them to remain looking exactly the same." Caroline's face registered fear and sadness.

Gretchen rose and bent over the back of Caroline's chair, kissing the top of her head and rubbing her mother's shoulders. "Who was she?"

Caroline went limp under Gretchen's fingers, giving herself over to the massage. "We met at a national doll convention long before I married your father. We kept in touch for a number of years, then lost track of each other, but every once in a while, I'd get news and see pictures of her fantasy dolls. Her name was Allison Thomasia." Caroline smiled, remembering.

"I wonder what happened in the cemetery," Gretchen said, feeling her mother's muscles tighten again, sorry she had said anything.

"Matt told me someone struck her several times, crushing her head. The murder weapon hasn't been found." Caroline's voice cracked.

Gretchen thought of the blood stains on the desert floor and Matt's observation that the woman had crawled before collapsing. She'd keep that knowledge to herself.

"Did she live in Phoenix?" Gretchen asked.

"I doubt it, or I would have heard."

The doorbell at the front of the house

rang. Gretchen heard Nimrod, the family gatekeeper, raising the alarm from inside.

"It's Matt," Gretchen said. "Nimrod will shake him down."

"We're around back," Caroline called out. A minute later Matt unlatched the outer patio door, came through, and placed a bag on the table. Nimrod burst back outside and tried to crawl up his leg. Matt reached down and stroked the little dog, greeted Caroline, then addressed Gretchen.

"Too lazy to properly greet the man of your dreams," he said. "I expected you to rush to me."

"I'm paralyzed with pleasure," Gretchen responded. "I can't move a single muscle."

"We'll have to work on your welcomes." He kissed her.

Gretchen loved the casual banter between them. He was a completely different person when he relaxed — fun, witty, sensual.

She walked into the house and went down the hall to get Daisy, but found her sprawled on the bed, talking on her cell. She refused to budge. "I couldn't eat a thing," Daisy said. "I'm too excited."

The rest of them dined on Gretchen's favorite food — green chile stew from Richardson's Restaurant. While they ate she thought about her plan for their evening mountain hike. She'd packed a light blanket, two wineglasses, candles, and a bottle of champagne. Tonight, she was going to have him all to herself. She had briefly considered faking a twisted ankle at the very height of Camelback to keep him up there. But knowing him, he'd call in a helicopter for a mountain rescue or attempt to carry her down. She'd better stay honest, if she didn't want him to heft her over his shoulder and find out that she wasn't a waif like his ex-wife.

"Let's go," Gretchen said when they finished, ready to implement her romantic plan.

"Gretchen, I'm very sorry, but I can't," Matt said. "As much as I want to, I'm working tonight. I was lucky to get away long enough to have dinner with you."

Gretchen's excitement transformed into major disappointment. She couldn't speak.

"Was the information I gave you helpful?" Caroline said after glancing at Gretchen and seeing her distress. "Did you locate Allison's husband?"

"Very much. At first we couldn't track him down — they had a home together in LA, but he wasn't there. Then he came into the station a little while ago to report his wife missing."

"Andy couldn't have taken the news well," Caroline said. "Those two were inseparable. I'd like to talk to him. Do you know where he's staying?"

"With us for the moment."

Caroline gasped. "You're holding him? The man found out moments ago that his wife is dead and you have him in custody?"

"We have procedures, Caroline. I don't make up the rules."

"I'm going down there immediately."

Matt shook his head. "That isn't possible. But I promise to notify you when he's released."

He had that all-business attitude that Gretchen was learning to recognize. She could almost see his mind working when he said, "According to him, they were vacationing in Phoenix. Yet it took the guy almost twenty-four hours to notify the police that his wife had disappeared. That's a long time, Caroline."

"You can't possibly suspect Andy?"

"Everyone is a suspect until we can prove otherwise." Matt stood up. "It was a pleasure, as always."

Gretchen walked with him along the side of the house, steering the conversation away from murder and on to safer ground by relating Nina's escapade in the haunted museum and her mission to find a ghost's doll.

Matt put his hands up and crossed his index fingers as if to ward off evil. "Don't tell me any more. I'm getting sweaty just hearing about d-o-l-l-s. That fairy doll almost put me over the edge."

Gretchen wrapped her fingers tightly through his. "I've been thinking about that poor woman's final moments," she said. "I can feel them as though they were my own."

"Once you see a murder scene it stays with you a long time."

Gretchen thought her last image of the victim might be around forever. "I'd like to help, if I can."

"Thanks, but you don't need to worry about my cases. Tell you what," Matt said. "I'll figure out who killed Allison Thomasia and you find out more about the ghost in the museum. Our time together is so short these days, let's not waste it with shoptalk. Ok?"

One sweet kiss and he was off, leaving Gretchen frustrated and pretty sure that he'd just told her to mind her own business.

11

The woman at the front door is like an all-terrain vehicle, solid, strong, rugged, in high gear as though she's had too much coffee. She's wearing a tentlike yellow top and matching cotton pants and white crew socks with leather sandals. He's annoyed by her presence this early in the day, having expected an opportunity to check out the hall before anyone arrived. He wants to shout out loud to blow off his building tension, but he's too smart for that. He holds it in.

"You just saved the show," she says all enthusiastic, reaching into his personal space. At first, he thinks she is going to bear-hug him, she's so excited. So he steps back, dodging, but she's only extending her hand. He doesn't want to touch her, but he needs to fit in. They shake. "I'm April," she says. "And you say you have experience with lighting?"

He gives her a short nod, and she claps

her hands together, like her prayers have been answered.

"That guy said you were looking for someone," he says, swinging his head toward the man standing at the street corner. The big guy doesn't cross the road in either direction. Instead he lights a pipe and loiters at the crosswalk. Who smokes a pipe these days?

"That's Mr. B. He owns this banquet hall," she says, squinting toward the pipe smoker over the top of her reading glasses, the sun hot and bright on her round face. "He lives upstairs. Good thing I mentioned to Mr. B. that we needed someone to do our lights, otherwise he wouldn't have passed it on to you. What a break for us."

"I was an electrician before I retired," he says. *Yeah, right.*

"What's your name?"

"Jerome." He doesn't try to think of an alias. It doesn't matter now and it won't matter later. He smells pipe tobacco, a light aroma of cherries, coming from Mr. B., who is greeting a woman walking by. He should get inside before the man decides to join them and says something to make this April woman suspicious.

"Why are we still standing here?" she says as though plucking his thoughts from his brain. "Come on in."

They enter the building and go down a hall to a banquet room, their footsteps echoing like thunder in a canyon. Dolls and teddy bears are in display cases on a stage; a heap of pink material is on a sewing machine. No one else around but the woman. And a small, nasty creature like a rat, that barrels at him. It snarls.

If it keeps coming, he'll kick it. The woman must sense his intention because she grabs it when it rushes by her to attack him.

"A local theater group is letting us use their stuff," she says, tucking the animal under an arm and leading him to a corner where lighting equipment is boxed, the flaps open like they looked inside but realized right away that this job was beyond them. One long black cord hangs out of a cardboard box.

"I better get busy stringing lights and running power." He doesn't have a clue how to start, but it can't be that hard. Hang them over the stage — the hooks are already in place he sees — focus the beams, flick them on and off at the right times. Not rocket science, and he's a smart guy.

"Where's the script?" At least he knows to ask. He should study it.

"I suppose that would help," she says digging through papers on a small table, finding what she's looking for, unbelievable considering the mess. "The director will be here soon. She can answer any questions you have. I made a pot of coffee if you want some."

She's at the sewing machine, making room among the folds of fabric to find her chair, muttering to the dog, tucking it into a bag hanging from the chair, picking up a pair of scissors. "Here," she says, coming at him with the scissors pointed right at him. "Let me take care of that for you." Right then he thinks he will have to hurt her. He doesn't have much time to consider his options. Before he pulls out his own weapon, she says, "I do that all the time. Leave tags on new clothes. Let me snip it off."

Jerome relaxes slightly, hand still stuffed in his pocket, gripping his switchblade just in case. He is taking a chance, letting someone get behind his back. She's quick. Holds the price tag up so he can see. Goes back to her machine.

That was close.

He helps himself to a cup of coffee before tackling the boxes of equipment. His first captured bird pops in his head, just like that, for no reason. When he was a kid he liked to sneak up on birds. He'd wait patiently, motionless, then strike like lightning. The first time, he took the bird home in his backpack, proud of his accomplishment. His mother wigged out, made him release it.

"That's not normal behavior," she said. "You should be playing ball with the rest of the kids."

But birds, he discovered, were much better companions than people.

He gulps the last dregs of coffee, wipes his mouth, and gets to work.

12

The majority of metal-head dolls were made in Germany, although some came from the United States and France. Metal heads were primarily produced from 1861 to the mid-1920s. Materials ranged from copper and zinc to brass, pewter, tin, lead, and aluminum. Gold and silver were used in rare and valuable cases. The heads were nearly indestructible. Metal doll heads could be purchased through Sears, Roebuck and Company, and Montgomery Ward until the early 1930s.

— From *World of Dolls* by Caroline Birch

Thursday morning Gretchen was on her first round of exercises on the Curves circuit when the subject of the haunted house came up, thanks to Nina, who couldn't concentrate on anything else.

And Gretchen had thought her aunt's

fascination with tarot cards had been intense!

"April's not here," Nina pointed out unnecessarily, suspiciously. "She isn't at the museum, is she? I don't want anyone over there. I made it quite clear."

Bonnie glanced up from the abductor machine. "She's at the banquet hall finishing up her sewing project."

Aside from Gretchen, her aunt, and Matt's mother, the only other women in Curves at the moment were Julie and Ora, the manager. The doll collectors had studied the crowd patterns and had picked a time to exercise when they had more space and privacy.

"What a relief," Nina said. "Thank goodness we aren't planning to open the museum to the public soon. I don't want anyone near the place until I get to the bottom of our problem."

"April thinks your ghost is really a genie," Bonnie said. "She wants to rub the travel trunk to see what happens."

Nina frowned. "She's still on that kick? I can't decide if she's making fun of me or not. April doesn't have any experience with ghosts. She isn't qualified to make a statement like that. Genies! That's ridiculous."

Gretchen could have mentioned that April

had as many credentials as Nina, which were none at all. Nor was she going to tell Nina that Caroline had left before sunrise to work at the very place that Nina was warning them to avoid. Bonnie and Julie knew, too, but were sworn to secrecy.

"An apparition is a very serious phenomenon," Nina said, running in place on a mat. "It's the disfranchised body of a displaced person, stuck between this plane and another one. We have to help her get unstuck so she can finish her journey."

"How did you actually see a ghost?" Ora called from the front desk. "Aren't they supposed to be invisible?"

Bonnie nodded her bewigged head. "I'm wondering the same thing."

"I thought I heard a sound coming from the vicinity of the trunk," Nina said, continuing on to the next machine. "Once I opened the lid, something swished past. I felt it touch my cheek on the flyby. It was very cold and silver. Yes, it absolutely, positively was silver."

"Why don't you go back and photograph it?" Bonnie said.

"That's a good idea," Nina said. "I'm one hundred percent sure I was touched by an apparition and it has something to do with the girl and her travel doll. Want to see a

96

picture of Flora when she was young? I remembered to bring it."

Everybody did.

The familiar programmed voice reminded them to switch stations while Blondie belted out "One Way or Another" from a speaker on the wall. Nina left the circle, dug through her purse on a shelf by the entrance, and came back with a sheet of paper. "The historical society people wouldn't let me take the actual photograph out of the building, but they made a copy of it."

She handed the sheet of paper to Gretchen. "That's her father, John Swilling. And that's Flora."

An unsmiling man with dark, neatly parted hair stared at the camera. He sat next to a young girl. Flora wore a chiffon dress with ribbons and a large bow on the right side of her short, dark bob. She held a doll in her arms. Part of the travel trunk was visible in the corner of the frame, not all of it, but enough to tell that it was the same trunk from the museum.

"Let me see," Julie said.

Gretchen passed the photo to her.

"A metal-head doll," Bonnie said, viewing the photo from behind Julie. "Those metal-head dolls really held up well, much better than porcelain," Bonnie continued, giving

Nina a lesson in doll history. "Too bad the paint they used in those days wasn't better quality. You can't find a metal head today that doesn't need major repainting. The heads were sold separately from the bodies, did you know that? And some were made from tin."

"And a cloth body," Gretchen said. "Probably homemade, as most of them were in the 1920s." Since working with her mother, Gretchen's doll knowledge had improved tremendously. She'd recently repainted a metal-head doll, and the owner had liked her work.

"Just like a bunch of doll collectors," Nina said, not sounding pleased at all. "The first thing you notice is the doll. Keep the picture, Gretchen. I made extras."

"I wouldn't try to take a picture of the ghost," Julie said. "What if it's a bad ghost?"

"I don't think ghosts can be bad," Nina said, looking unsure.

Until recent events, Gretchen hadn't had strong personal opinions on any of Nina's past delvings — tarot cards, auras, her conversations with the universe, the telepathic communications she'd tried to share with Gretchen with limited and questionable success. Throughout all of it, Gretchen usually had a wait-and-see attitude.

"I heard," she said to the doll collectors, "that almost half of the population believes in ghosts."

"And one in five has seen a ghost," Nina added. "Ghost hunters have documented sightings that have been verified by other people who were with them at the time."

Unlike colored auras and Nina's other pursuits that were all based on her testimony alone, ghost sightings were group activities. Was there truth in numbers?

Gretchen didn't know and she wasn't sure she wanted to find out. It was exciting to think about, though.

The cemetery murder came up next. Gretchen had made a point of avoiding the subject. Since Bonnie was Matt's mother and the club's biggest gossip, all Matt needed to hear was that Gretchen was discussing his cases with his mother and her other workout buddies.

She needn't have bothered, though, since Bonnie chimed in with, "My Matty is working on a tough case, a murder in Eternal View Cemetery. He can't tell me a thing about it, because it's highly confidential. However, my friend Anne works in the office at the cemetery and she gave me all the gory details."

Bonnie's red wig was adjusted properly

for a change, and her penciled eyebrows were straight. Recently she'd switched to half-decaf, half-regular coffee. It had been Nina's suggestion, a "psychic moment" she called it, and the results were amazing. No more jitters for Bonnie. No more crooked wigs or wobbly eyebrows. "Want to hear the details?" she asked.

"My. More juicy gossip," Ora said. "You girls are energized today."

Gretchen was all ears. Anything she could learn might help solve the crime and put a killer away. And as an added benefit, getting the case wrapped up quickly would get Matt back in her arms with his mind focused completely on her.

"We're ready, Bonnie," Nina said. "Don't leave out a thing."

"Well, Gretchen was there when it happened," Bonnie said. "She should help tell it."

"Really?" Julie said, swinging her head toward Gretchen in surprise.

"What?" Nina shouted. "Is that true? I'm family. Why am I always the last to know anything?"

"I'm sorry, Nina." *Thank you, Bonnie.* "It was so late by the time I got home . . ." What else could she say?

"My own niece," Nina said. "Absolutely

no consideration for me at all."

Bonnie jumped in again. "I knew Gretchen had been there the minute Anne said the detective had a woman with him."

"Was your friend Anne in the cemetery when it happened?" Gretchen asked.

"No, but she was behind on her work, so she stayed late in the office that night. She was going to her car when she heard a ruckus in the cemetery. She's the one who called the cops. Of course, she didn't know about the dead woman until the police arrived and searched the area."

Two other Curves members came through the door, putting an end to their private conversation. "Let's stretch," Bonnie said, leading them to another room. Gretchen took up the end position. They were like a flock of inquisitive turkeys all in a row, trotting along with their necks craned.

Nina hadn't said a word since she found out that Gretchen had been in the cemetery and hadn't told her. She was too busy showing Gretchen that she was angry by ignoring her. "I'm sorry," Gretchen mouthed the next time Nina glared her way. No reaction from her aunt.

Bonnie was already sitting on a floor mat, twisting over one raised knee. "Here's the scoop. It wasn't a random murder. A bunch of those homeless people were lurking in the cemetery, so that would have been my first thought, that one of them did it, or all of them together."

Gretchen couldn't imagine Nacho or Daisy killing anyone or anything. She'd have to take Bonnie down to the rescue mission for a little charitable giving. "People everywhere come in all kinds of packages," she said. "Good and evil exists on all social levels."

"But that's what the police would have thought," Bonnie continued. "That she had been picked just because she was in the wrong place at the wrong time, or because she reminded the killer of someone, or because of whatever reason a psycho kills. But that wasn't the case because the police found a big clue."

"What big clue?" Julie asked.

"A doll," Bonnie said. Gretchen made a point of keeping her mouth shut.

Everyone had forgotten to stretch. Instead they huddled together like football players. Bonnie continued in a whisper. "I put two and two together when Anne told me the dead woman's name. Allison Thomasia. I searched on the Internet and found her right away. She was a fantasy doll artist."

"My mother knew her," Gretchen said

quietly. "They were old friends but had lost touch over the years."

"What was Allison doing in the cemetery?" Nina asked. Gretchen took it as a good sign that the intrigue was winning her aunt over enough that she hadn't even commented on Caroline's connection to the dead woman.

"No one knows," Bonnie said. "Or if they do, they aren't saying. I'm going to keep at Matty, but my son has tight lips."

Since learning he can't trust his mother to keep a secret, Gretchen thought.

"What I want to know," Nina said, "is whose grave was she visiting after dark?"

All eyes turned to Gretchen, who shrugged.

"Gretchen doesn't know," Nina said, still testy. "Right there at the scene of the crime and she doesn't notice the engraving on the headstone."

"She must have been very upset," Julie said in Gretchen's defense.

"It was pitch-black," Gretchen said. "And, yes, I was upset." *When was the last time you stood beside a murdered woman?* "The woman had crawled from one location to another. I really don't know the answer, but that's a very good question."

"Fine," Nina snapped. "A killer is on the loose, killing doll collectors, which all of

you happen to be, and you didn't notice.
Fine. Just fine."

13

What is the difference between antique dolls and vintage dolls?

Dates!

Dolls produced prior to 1930 are considered antiques. Most antique dolls came from European countries, especially France and Germany. The dolls were clothed in Victorian and Edwardian fashions. Today they serve as delightful historical artifacts.

Vintage dolls were designed between 1930 and 1980, and were produced by doll manufacturers such as the Alexander Doll Company, Ideal Toy and Novelty Company, and Mattel, among others.

— From *World of Dolls* by Caroline Birch

Caroline unpacks boxes in the museum's upstairs storage room, the same room in which her sister claimed she'd witnessed the presence of an apparition. Nina has made her aware of every creak and groan from the old home, thanks to her talk of otherworldly creatures. Nina has always been very different from Caroline, searching for answers best left unfound, those that defy human logic.

Caroline has never been able to decide if Nina is right or wrong. Strange things *do* happen when she is around. Unexplainable things. But Caroline is more comfortable with her black-and-white view of the world. Why complicate it any more than it already is by throwing in beings from other worlds and other dimensions?

She glances at her watch. Ten o'clock a.m., still enough time to look through one more box of dolls before heading home to meet with a customer. The cast of *Ding Dong Dead* should be at the banquet hall deep into rehearsal. Caroline is very glad she opted out of that fiasco, preferring to work quietly and at her own pace at the museum. She's also glad that she didn't let the other members talk her into trying to open the museum this month. She needs three, four, maybe five months, hopefully less once the luncheon and play are over, when the others can devote more time to help prepare the museum's displays.

She withdraws dolls from storage containers, one at a time, unwraps them, examining each to determine if it needs repair. Some are antiques, some vintage. Most of the dolls have been preserved well, packed away with expert care. Little is required other than smoothing a wrinkled costume here and there, recurling a lock of hair, wiping a smudge away, finding the proper stand. She has a few of her supplies at hand for the most simple repairs.

The next item that she unwraps is a metal doll head. The doll head has yellow painted hair, red lips, enormous blue painted eyes. The face paint is chipped away in spots, leaving marks like white chicken pox. Caroline isn't surprised to be holding a head without a body. Many of the metal-head dolls were sold that way, and the new owner would then find a suitable body. She wonders about the body this one might have had. Metal, wooden, kid leather, cloth? She works her way through the rest of the container's contents without finding an unattached body.

The paint she needs to restore the doll face is at home in her repair workshop. She'll take the head with her when she leaves, find time when it becomes available. There is no rush. One doll head won't be missed. The collection is enormous, and this isn't even one of the most rare or valuable types of metal heads.

Caroline rewraps it in the original packing paper, puts it into a white plastic bag, and places it in a shopping bag with several other dolls needing work. Then she locks the museum's door and drives toward home, thinking of the customer she's about to meet.

The call came from a man who has never used her service before, but is excessively demanding, wanting a rapid repair in spite of his tenuous position as a first-time client. She should have refused, but he pressed hard and the financial reward offered for quick service was too high to turn down.

She weaves through the gridlock traffic. It's always rush hour in Phoenix, too many people, too few lanes, the new highway systems becoming jammed as soon as they are built. Camelback Mountain is in sight and beckons to her as always, a calming natural force in the mass of humanity.

The traffic frees, and she quickens her pace.

A white van pulls up alongside her at a red light, blocking her view on the right side. Again. She notices it because it seems to pace her; whether she speeds up or slows down, the van is right there at her side. It's beat-up, junky, most of the side panel damaged, dented and rusty. The vehicle's windows are heavily tinted, privacy windows.

She has room ahead to speed up and rid herself of the van. She does, but the van does the same.

Jerk! She hates driving in the city, the rudeness and unpredictability. The games of chicken. *Look at me, I'm king of the road.* Everybody driving massive SUVs, one-upping each other in size and power.

The white van is almost in her lane, veering over the line, forcing her closer to the center where cars rush at her from the opposite direction. A horn blares. An oncoming car swerves. She weaves, then returns to her lane.

What a close call!

"Take it easy. Get in your own lane!" she shouts out loud even though the van driver can't possibly hear her. Her heart is thumping.

The van still paces her. Either the van driver is drunk or distracted by a phone call or something equally inattentive and dangerous. She glances over to see the side of the van within inches of striking her car. Now it is her turn to lay on the horn, a shrill plea to the other driver to pay attention, the flat of her hand hitting the horn hard.

Instead of moving off, the van lurches at her, sharply, a wrenching at her as though they are playing roller derby and are adversaries. A solid hit.

She feels the impact and grips the wheel with both hands, struggling to control the car, intuitively knowing that her efforts are wasted. She uses every muscle in her body, focuses with all the power in her being, but still the car swerves beneath her, heading the wrong way.

Then another impact that should have been head-on, but her car has a life of its own and is turned sideways when the collision occurs. She sees the woman's face up close, too close, horrified, mouth open in alarm as she plows into the passenger side of Caroline's car.

Oncoming cars are running into the other woman's car from behind, sending them both spinning. Glass breaks. The sound is loud, louder than she could ever have imagined. Her neck is wrenched. She feels a sharp pain, but it doesn't matter. Nothing matters at the moment, because time is suspended. It has ceased to exist.

Caroline closes her eyes. There's nothing more she can do to save herself. She feels her world turn upside down.

14

Gretchen watched Matt get out of his car holding a bouquet of flowers. He sprinted into the banquet hall without seeing her approaching from the coffee shop down the street. *Some detective,* she thought with a smile. Coffee in hand, she perched on the front of his car and waited for him to come back out, not wanting to share him with the others.

The sun still felt like an old friend this early in May, but it would start to sizzle and scorch the desert by June, at the latest.

Julie came rushing along the street, her haphazard updo as messy as ever. She stopped when she saw Gretchen. "What are you doing on top of that car?"

She must look foolish! "It's Matt's car. He's inside. He'll be right out."

"Hope I'm not too late."

"Bonnie's been working on her lines. You're fine. Don't tell Matt I'm out here."

Julie looked puzzled but willing. "I won't." She slipped into the hall.

After several more minutes, Matt came out of the building and was startled to find her lounging on the hood of his car.

"What's this?" he said, fistful of roses whipped behind his back. "You knew I was taking my life into my hands by going into this building and you didn't warn me?"

"You mean because of your doll problem?" Gretchen pretended not to notice the flowers. "You must like me a lot to risk the sight of all those Barbie dolls on the stage."

"I didn't know the stage setting was in place, or I never would have gone in, even for you." He offered his free hand in a gallant gesture to help her alight from his vehicle. She accepted. "But I really meant those women. I'm lucky I got out with my clothes still on my body."

"They are a scary bunch."

"My mother appeared from a back room just in time to save my clothes, but calling me Matty in front of everyone was thoroughly embarrassing."

"Yup. She always calls you Matty. And the rest of them are man-starved."

"One of them pointed a gun at me."

"Tsk. You poor thing. Want to escape to my secret hideout until we're sure it's safe to come out?"

He glanced at the door to the building. "Absolutely."

"What's behind your back?"

He presented the roses. A dozen vibrant red roses resting in baby's breath.

The first time in years that Gretchen had received flowers from a man.

"Please don't tell me I made you cry." Matt looked worried.

"No. Thank you. I love them. What's the occasion?"

"Our four-month anniversary."

"Oh, okay." Had it really been four months since his divorce was finalized? Since the day they had met on the mountain, at the halfway point?

"Run," he said playfully. "Quick! The door is opening. They're going to get me."

Gretchen turned to see that no one was following them before they trotted down the street, laughing like kids.

This Great Coffee Place was her favorite coffee shop. A Costa Rican light roast and one of the shop's scones was a small slice of heaven on earth. Matt ordered a cup of coffee, and Joan, the friendly proprietor, topped off Gretchen's cup.

"Great flowers," someone called out.

"You must have said yes," from someone else.

"Way to go, Gretchen."

Matt led her to the most private table he could find.

"You know everyone in here," he commented, taking the bouquet from her and laying it on the side of the table. "Is this where you hang out on a regular basis?"

"It's comfortable, has positive energy, and is convenient when I can't stand working with the cast any longer."

"That bad?"

"Worse." Gretchen cut a chocolate chip scone in half and nibbled on tiny pieces of it. "What happened with Andy Thomasia?"

"Under investigation, top secret."

"So he's the prime suspect?"

"Spouses, lovers, they always start out at the top of my list."

"Nina thinks you're dealing with a killer who goes after doll collectors."

A small smile crept over his lips. He was always greatly amused by her aunt's unusual take on life. "Nina would think that."

"Tell me what you've found so far." Gretchen leaned across the table. "That is, unless it isn't any of my business."

"I value your opinion mightily." He leaned in to meet her. He kissed her nose, sending a bolt of electricity through her body. How would she react when they got past a few lip-locks? That unleashed bolt of power might kill her.

Matt sat back. "LAPD is assisting. The victim had a small studio in her Los Angeles home where she made dolls. The artistry of the doll found at the crime scene is consistent with her other works. Did you know that Allison and Andy Thomasia were estranged at the time of her death?"

"No." Gretchen's mother would be interested in that bit of news.

"She remained in their LA home. He rented an apartment. Recently, according to him, they were in the process of reconciling. He claims she invited him along to Phoenix. He'd hoped to work things out between them while here."

"What about the homeless people in the cemetery?"

"No help at all so far."

"Did you let all of them go?" Gretchen was thinking specifically of Nacho.

"What a mess that was." Matt studied his coffee cup as though remembering every detail with dread. "Seventeen potential witnesses without a single one of them admitting having heard or seen a thing. No drivers' licenses, no state ID cards, no other

115

kind of identification on any of them. All we could do was put them through the paces — photographs, fingerprints. We let them go." He looked up at her. "You know some of those people. Maybe you can get them to talk to you?"

"I tried. I haven't seen Nacho, but Daisy claims she didn't see or hear a thing, so they're sticking with their story. Maybe they're telling the truth." A thought occurred to her. "Wait . . . does this mean you need me?"

"I always need you, baby."

"I thought I was supposed to mind my own business."

"I never said that."

Men!

"You implied it."

"Ahh, those nasty implications."

"Tell me again that you need my help."

"I," Matt said with a great grin, "need your help. But only this one time."

Gretchen heard sirens in the distance, not an uncommon sound in one of the most congested cities in the country with a large, aging population. Sirens were as routinely heard as other traffic noises, yet the sound always reminded Gretchen of disaster. The sirens gave her pause to reflect on how lucky she was.

"By the way," Matt said. "There was a multiple-car accident near Twenty-fourth Street and Camelback. Stay clear of that area for a while."

15

At first Gretchen thought the object under her windshield wiper was a parking ticket. Until she pulled it loose. She unfolded it and stared in shock at the words.

Die, Dolly, Die.

The letters had been individually cut out of newspaper print and glued together in a semistraight line on a piece of white paper.

The same words that had been written on the gravestone.

A threat or a warning? A prediction of her future? Could Nina have left it to scare her into taking the tarot reading more seriously? No. Her aunt wouldn't go that far.

A prankster, maybe? The doll club members were known to pull practical jokes. But this one wasn't funny. Not one bit.

She looked up and down the sidewalk, scanning both sides of the street. What was she searching for exactly? A killer who targeted doll collectors as Nina had suggested? No one on either side of the street paid any attention to Gretchen. Those passing by seemed focused on their destinations, not on her reaction to a piece of paper. It had to be a bad joke.

Inside the banquet hall, the cast was on-stage, reading from their scripts, focusing much more intently than usual, which was highly suspicious. Their deep concentration had her convinced that they were up to something.

"Who put this on my car?" Gretchen demanded, waving the paper in one hand, clutching the roses in the other. "And don't pretend that you don't know what I'm talking about."

"Shhh," April whispered from Gretchen's director's chair. "Can't you see we're in the middle of rehearsal? And I think they've finally got it down pat. Keep going, crew." She rose and grabbed Gretchen by the arm, pulling her away from the stage and guiding her into the break room. "Don't stop them now. They're on a roll." She looked proud of herself. "All it took was a little tantalizing incentive. Speaking of tantalizing, where's that hot, sexy man of yours?"

"Gone back to the job. Listen, I have to talk to the cast."

"Nice flowers." April took the bouquet

and placed the flowers into a tall water glass. "You can talk to them, but you can't just barge in. They'll be through with this act in a few minutes. Don't you want to know what motivated them?"

"What incentive could possibly have Bonnie speaking her lines correctly?"

April tackled a box of glazed donuts, popping a donut hole in her mouth and chewing it quickly before answering. "When they came in this morning after their Curves workout, Bonnie couldn't talk about anything but the cemetery murder. I told her if she could get through the play, front to back, without any mistakes, you would take her to the scene of the crime."

"What? I didn't agree to that."

"I took creative license." April, another donut in hand, stuck her head out the door before continuing. "Just listen to them."

Even though the cast were still reading from scripts, rather than off-book, they sounded much better than Gretchen could have ever hoped for after the last several disastrous days. "I have to admit, they sound pretty good."

"See?"

"Who would have thought a trip to a cemetery would be Bonnie's carrot?" Gretchen wished she had thought of something so clever.

"They're going to make it through every scene without screwing up," April said. "But the others don't want to go along. They're only working hard for Bonnie because it means so much to her."

"I'm not sure if I want them to make it. Going to a cemetery right after a murder isn't exactly my ideal afternoon outing. Besides, I just found a note —"

"Oh come on," April said, interrupting. "You have to. Look at them."

Gretchen watched as the cast worked away. She could see how hard Bonnie was trying. "Tell her we'll go to the cemetery later this afternoon," she said, defeated.

What had she gotten herself into? More important at the moment, was she cut out for directorship? Should she trade positions with April, sit at the sewing machine, and watch her friend take over?

"What's that?" April noticed the paper in Gretchen's hand.

Gretchen gave it to her.

"*Die, Dolly, Die.* Not a bad title," April said. "But don't you like the one we already have? *Ding Dong Dead* has a nice ring to it, and we sent out invitations using it."

A play title? April thought it was an idea for a different title? "It was stuck on my windshield wiper blade," Gretchen said. "I thought it was a joke or prank of some sort, but you didn't even know."

"Know what?"

"Nothing. It's nothing." She realized with increasing concern that she hadn't told the club members about the horrible words on the headstone. Not even Bonnie knew about that; if she had, it would have been the first thing she mentioned. The police were keeping it quiet.

"I like the one Caroline came up with better," April said. She scrunched the paper and tossed it into the garbage can before Gretchen could stop her. She would have to dig it out before she left to show it to Matt.

They stood in the doorway and watched the rehearsal. A man wearing gray overalls came out from behind the stage. He unrolled a black extension cord as he backed up. "Who's that?"

"Jerome. He's our new lighting expert."

The man produced a roll of duct tape from a deep pocket. He squatted and began covering the electrical cord, taping it to the floor.

"Where did you find him?" April was turning out to be a competent general manager, even though her original title had been seamstress and donut runner. She was a woman of many talents, and Gretchen wasn't about to waste those talents on gofer runs.

"I plucked him right off the street." April giggled. "Well, not really. Mr. B. recommended him."

"Great. Where's Nina?"

"Oops."

"Oops?"

"You weren't supposed to be back from your morning date with Hot Man yet."

"Something's up."

April looked guilty. "Nina's walking the dogs," she said. "Please don't be mad. I couldn't leave Enrico home alone."

"April, we had one rule and one rule only: no pets."

"I know, I know. It won't happen again." The new light technician had noticed Gretchen and was heading over. April dropped her voice and redirected the conversation. "Don't call Jerome names. He gets really mad."

Gretchen whispered back. "What kind of names?"

"Like Sparky or Lampy or Noodle Tech. Oh, look, here he comes."

Jerome stood silently while April introduced him. She talked him up, describing his contribution in the most glowing terms possible. He shuffled uncomfortably, watching his feet, while April laid out his achievements. At first Gretchen thought he was self-conscious, not used to compliments.

A flash of icy steel in his eyes when he finally looked at her informed her otherwise. After he went back to work, Gretchen said, "Not the friendliest guy."

April shrugged. "He's doing his job, free of charge I might add. He's a volunteer. Lighten up."

"How is he getting along with the cast?"

"Fine."

Gretchen thought she detected something in April's tone, but why should she worry herself about every little detail? Whatever April was doing was working.

"Would you mind directing for a few more days?"

"Gee, no, not at all. I really like it."

"That'll give me time to catch up on a few repair jobs."

"Don't feel bad that I'm doing a better job than you are," April said. "Our minds work differently. Mine's just better suited to this line of work than yours is."

"What do you mean?"

"Well, for example, look at your director's desk."

"What's wrong with it?"

"It's a mess. Papers scattered everywhere, old coffee getting moldy in cups."

What could she say? April wasn't lying. The proof was right in front of them.

"I never pretended to be a neat freak," Gretchen said.

"Directing a play takes a lot of organizational skills. Creative people, like you, don't compartmentalize like accounting types."

"You aren't an accounting type." April's home furnishings were topsy-turvy, every single bit of space taken up with something.

"Yes, but I make up for it by having an excess of managerial skills. You know what you should be doing?"

Spending time with Matt, Gretchen thought.

"You should be creating museum displays," April said. "I suggest that I take over your job. You take over mine."

April had a point. Hadn't Gretchen wished for that same thing, to help out at the museum instead? "Let me think about it," she said.

After promising to meet them at the cemetery later in the afternoon, depending on April's assessment of their performance, Gretchen returned to the break room to retrieve the note from the trash.

She bumped into Jerome as he was coming out. When he looked into her eyes, she sensed his coldness again. She gave him a weak smile.

What a creepy guy!

After pulling every single item out of the garbage, Gretchen gave up.

The note was gone.

16

It takes several hours to extricate all of the victims from the crumpled cars and to clear the street of scattered debris. Firefighters, paramedics, police officers, and equipment contribute to rescue efforts. The team cuts away whole sections of cars to get at victims trapped beneath steering wheels or pinned against crushed dashboards, prying open vehicles like giant tins of tuna. They are professionals, and they work quickly and quietly. Everyone has a job and knows exactly how to accomplish it.

Caroline is bloody, but other than superficial wounds, most of the blood is from others. She doesn't have time to think of herself. She reacts instinctively, offering comfort and reassurances to the other victims.

By the time Matt Albright arrives, those involved in the five-car accident have been extricated and transported to the hospital.

One woman is already at the morgue after having been pronounced dead at the scene. Caroline watches Matt scan the wreckage before his eyes find her. She is sitting on the curb next to her car, which is upside down. The windows are blown out. A cop sweeps up the last shards of auto glass.

Emergency vehicles are still on the scene, although the ambulances are gone. Several tow trucks idle while the drivers load crumpled cars onto flatbeds.

"Are you okay?" Matt squats beside her, his dark eyes penetrating her own.

"Other than a sore neck, yes."

"Let's have you checked out." He rises and stops the officer in charge, who has chosen this moment to walk past them. "Why wasn't she transported? Get an ambulance. *Now!*"

"I refused," she says. "It isn't his fault. Others needed it more than I did."

Matt doesn't respond, although she can tell that he is upset. Instead, he confers with the officer.

"One dead," the cop says. "The rest? Multiple injuries, a crushed pelvis, head wounds, et cetera."

"Any kids?" Matt asks.

Caroline hates when children are involved in accidents and sees Matt's relief when the officer shakes his head. No kids.

"This is what's left of the vehicle that started the chain reaction." They stare at Caroline's car. Matt crouches and ducks his head to peer inside. A few items are on the roof of the car, which is now the floor.

Until this moment, Caroline has been too busy helping others to consider her own situation. She begins to tremble slightly.

"I'll put your personal belongings in my car," Matt says. "Once your car is towed away, retrieving contents will be more difficult."

Caroline nods.

"Plenty of witnesses to the accident," the officer says while waving one of the tow trucks through. "According to them a white van sideswiped the vehicle, this woman lost control, jumped the median, ended up in oncoming traffic, going the wrong way. Nobody coming at her is paying enough attention, talking on their cell phones, et cetera. So they pile up, one after the other. She manages to roll the car — sorry, lady, but don't even ask me how — and it spins over this way, taking out the Mini Cooper." His arms are flying back and forth across the lanes of traffic, which have been reopened. Cars are passing slowly by, passengers gawking at them, trying to get a grasp on the events that led to this chaos.

"Where's the van?" Matt asks, surveying the lane closest to the curb, the lane still closed off to traffic.

"Hit and run." The officer has seen this before. Caroline can hear it in his voice. Witnesses got the plates, and we're tracking it down." He moves off.

Matt sits down on the curb. "Your family," he says, "is like a pride of cats, nine lives for each of you. How many have you used up so far?"

"Probably all of them."

Before he can respond, a truck goes past with what's left of the Mini Cooper. The car looks like shredded scrap metal.

"Look over there," Matt says.

Caroline's eyes sweep over the spectators. She sees a group on the other side of Camelback Road. Shoppers have parked in a shopping mall on her side and have wandered over to observe the final cleanup, ask around, find out what they missed. Matt is pointing out a few homeless individuals standing off by themselves.

"Nacho and Daisy aren't with them," he says. "Your two street friends are living just like the rest of those tortured souls who subsist on the fringes."

Caroline takes time to really study the

man sitting beside her. He is more complex than she once thought. Matt has allowed her a brief glimpse inside himself.

He smiles. "Anybody who matters to Gretchen matters to me. Now I'm committed to keeping them safe, if I can."

"Nacho was here earlier," Caroline says. "He checked to make sure I wasn't hurt, but then he disappeared. He's a difficult person for me to get to know."

"And Daisy isn't?"

Caroline smiles.

They sit in silence after that.

A man wearing gray overalls joins the indigents, but he doesn't really fit with them, although they seem to accept him. His clothes are clean, and he's not wearing layers and layers of them; he's trimmed up, good haircut, shaven. He doesn't stay more than a minute or two, probably asking what happened.

The street people always know, if you can get them to talk. They have a remarkable communication system, if she could only figure it out.

She takes another look at her car.

The officer in charge finishes another task and comes over to study the car, too. "She crawled out the busted-out window," he says to Matt as though she isn't there. "Had a little trouble getting the seat belt off, sitting upside down, et cetera, but she did it. Ended up helping some of the others."

"Did she now?" Matt smiles at Caroline again.

"That's one tough cookie." He walks away.

"Et cetera," Matt says.

Caroline should contact Gretchen, make sure she learns of the accident in a gentle manner. The death of her father is bound to make the news of this accident more frightening. Bring back memories best forgotten.

"I'm not going to make a big deal of my part in the accident," she says to Matt.

"It was a big deal."

"I mean when I tell Gretchen what happened. I wish I didn't have to tell her at all, but she'll notice the missing car." Caroline adds a hint of playfulness to her voice, practicing lightness for when she talks to her daughter. "Please don't say anything to her. Once she comes home and sees that I'm not hurt, it'll be easier for me to relate the facts as they really happened. I don't want her having bad memories of the accident she had with her father without my being there to comfort her."

"I'm not going to lie to Gretchen," he says.

"Then disappear for the rest of the day," Caroline says, and there is an edge to her voice. "Don't communicate with her."

"Are you sure you're all right?"

"I'm alive, which is more than can be said for that other woman."

"Call me if you need anything."

"I will, thanks."

"We're looking for the van."

"I'm sure you'll find it, but the driver has had plenty of time to disappear."

"You think it was intentional?"

"You want to know if I think someone was trying to kill me? I choose to believe it was an accidental collision. You'll tell me if you learn otherwise, right?"

"Yes, ma'am. I'll give you a lift in a few minutes."

Matt goes off to talk with a witness, then walks down the block to study the path of Caroline's car. Later, while driving her home, he gets a call.

"A stolen white van has been found abandoned on the other side of the city," he informs her.

"Don't tell Gretchen, at least not yet. I'll be careful. Let you know if anything unusual happens."

"You mean like another hit-and-run?"

"You are a sassy boy."

"And you're just like your daughter."

While she listens, he calls and orders an

officer to patrol her street.

"To keep an eye on the house," he explains to her. "Just in case."

17

April's white Lincoln was parked on the street outside of the cemetery entrance. Gretchen pulled up behind her, got out, and walked up to the car.

Bonnie was in the passenger seat. Julie sat alone in the back.

"Nina will be here in a few minutes," Gretchen said.

"Smart thinking," April said. "You would have been in big trouble if you left her out. Again."

Exactly! Gretchen wasn't going to subject herself to Nina's wrath unless she absolutely had to.

"Here she comes," Julie said.

Nina parked in the shade of an orange tree.

"Tutu can wait in the car with Enrico," Gretchen said to her aunt. "It's a nice day. She isn't going to roast."

"Why can't she come?"

April snorted. "She might wee-wee on the graves, that's why."

They piled into Gretchen's car, and she drove inside the cemetery gates.

"I love visiting cemeteries," April said from the backseat. "Especially old cemeteries. It's one of my hobbies. I can hardly wait."

"That's creepy," Nina said, turning her lithe body to glance into the back.

"And ghost chasing isn't?" April replied.

"I can't help it if I attract otherworldly beings," Nina said. "They gravitate to me because of my ability to communicate with them. It's not like I have a choice. They pick me. Flora's situation is a perfect example. She didn't show herself to anyone until I arrived, did she?"

"That's true," Bonnie said.

"Cemeteries are steeped in history," April said. "You get a flavor of the different eras and cultures when you take the time to read the headstones."

"My hunt to help a ghost is steeped in history, too," Nina reminded her.

Gretchen's hands were sweaty on the steering wheel. She stopped the car next to the same palm tree that she'd leaned against after running away from the dead woman's frozen stare.

The cemetery didn't look as forbidding in the light of day. Mountains framed the sky-scape, and ancient red earth spread underfoot. To Gretchen, the lack of greenery looked exotic, and the desert hues warmed her. Living in Arizona was like living on another planet, the smells and visuals so different from Boston where she had grown up.

Gretchen looked around — palm trees, several native shade trees, white crosses rising from tall grave markers, the sun glistening from metal grave sculptures and ornaments.

"Ever been to Tombstone?" April asked, hefting her body out of the back of Gretchen's car. "Boot Hill Cemetery is where many of the old-time western gunslingers are buried. One of my favorite tombstones says, 'Here lies Lester Moore/Four slugs from a 44/No les, no more.' "

The women stood outside the car. Julie hadn't said a word since getting out of April's car. Her dyed black hair looked harsh in the daylight. Both her and Bonnie's faces were pale.

"Are you feeling all right?" Gretchen asked them.

"I'm a little jittery," Julie said.

"Me, too," Bonnie agreed.

"If you ever get to Key West," April went on, "go to the old cemetery in the 'dead' of town." She elbowed Bonnie. "Pun intended. That's the spookiest cemetery and the most interesting. The graves are aboveground. The coffins are stacked on top of each other because the bedrock is too hard to dig into. One of the graves reads, "I told you I was sick.' "

"Shush," Nina said. "We have to show proper respect for the dead. And you're scaring Julie. Gretchen, lead the way."

"Over here." Gretchen retraced her steps as she remembered them. First to the tree, then at an angle to Matt.

An eerie silence permeated the spring air. A light breeze ruffled Gretchen's hair.

"Where is the first headstone?" Nina asked her. "You have a lost expression on your face, like you don't know where you are."

"It was dark. Let me see." Gretchen stopped and studied her car, parked where Matt's had been two nights ago. She visualized an imaginary line from the car to the palm tree, then to the lipstick-marked grave. "There." She had been off by only a few graves. The women followed her as she re-aligned.

There weren't any signs of lipstick markings anywhere. She still hadn't told her friends about the handwriting on the headstone. If Matt's intention was to keep that information from the public, she'd support him. But she wanted to ask him about it. She'd have to tell him about the note also.

April squinted over the top of her reading glasses. "William Hayden," she read. "Anybody know that name?"

They all agreed that they didn't.

"Sure are a lot of Haydens buried together," Bonnie observed.

April read off the names of others buried close by in case Gretchen was mistaken about the specific grave marker. None of the names sounded familiar to any of them.

"Show us where the body was found," April said.

Gretchen had been avoiding the spot, focusing her attention instead on the mountains in the distance or the gravel at her feet. Any place other than where Allison Thomasia's body had been discovered. When she forced herself to glance in that direction, she half expected to see a body, the blood, the stare. Instead she gazed at more of the same: red earth, white crosses, heavy marble headstones. Nothing to remind her of the other night except for the images seared in her memory.

"Right here," she said. The women formed a circle around the plot she was staring down at.

Cemetery protocol eluded her. Were they supposed to stay off of the graves? She thought the answer was yes. But how? Hard to do considering there weren't any obvious walkways between them.

April was standing right on top of the one she had indicated, scanning the ground over her glasses, looking for clues.

"The ground's soaked in blood," Bonnie announced, confirming Gretchen's silent opinion.

The sandstone earth *did* seem slightly redder over the grave. It wasn't Gretchen's imagination.

"Oh my Gawd," Nina said. "Get a load of this."

Gretchen turned to find Nina standing in front of one of the headstones.

"This is the same man who built the house," Nina said when April and Bonnie didn't make the connection.

But Gretchen had. "We've located John Swilling's grave."

"And his wife Emma is buried beside him," Nina said, reading the inscription aloud. "Wait." She pulled a small notepad from her purse and flipped through it. "I should have made a copy of the historical records instead of jotting notes, but how was I to know at the time?"

While her aunt went through her notes, Gretchen read the scant information on the gravestone. John Swilling had been forty-eight when he died in 1946, his wife even younger when she'd been placed in the cold hard earth. She'd been only twenty-four years old at the time and had died the same year the house was constructed. Births, names, deaths were the only part of their story that the gravestone gave away. Side by side for the rest of eternity.

"I thought so," Nina said. "Flora's birth record was in the files at the historical society. According to these dates" — she waved at the headstone — "Flora Swilling was born on the same day that Emma passed away. Emma must have died giving birth to Flora."

"How sad," Bonnie said. "She never knew her mother."

While her friends made sympathetic noises over a little girl who never had a chance to experience the comfort of her mother's arms, Gretchen walked away from the stone and stood at the foot of the graves.

There was space for at least one more

family member, maybe two.

"Is your friend working in the office today?" Gretchen asked Bonnie.

"I think so," Bonnie answered. "Let's go see."

"Let's leave," Julie said. "I've seen enough."

"I told you not to come," April said. "You're too nice."

"Thanks," Julie said. "I think."

Nina walked over, stopped beside Gretchen, and studied the graves from Gretchen's point of view. "Look at that!" she said after only a moment, leaving Gretchen to wonder again about her aunt's ability to tune into her own thoughts.

Aunt and niece looked at each other.

"A family plot," they said simultaneously.

"The cops have already been through all this," Bonnie's friend Anne said. Her arms were wedged into the top drawer of a filing cabinet. She pulled out a manila folder, shut the drawer, and sat down at her desk.

"Did my Matty check into this particular file specifically? You know, this one for Swilling?" Bonnie's pet name for her son had seemed endearing at first but was quickly starting to annoy Gretchen almost as much as it did Matt.

"There isn't a Swilling file, and I told them the same thing," Anne said. "Several officers went through all the files, the cabinet, and the computer records, like they didn't believe me." She withdrew a single sheet of paper from the file and leaned forward. "This is the extent of the records from the old cemetery. The rest burned up in a fire in the fifties."

"What is it?" Julie asked. Some of her color had returned since they'd left the graveyard and entered the office.

"It's a document from the Arizona Historical Preservation Office," Anne said. "The old cemetery has a historic designation. We can't remove any of the bodies."

"Would you want to?" Julie asked, losing her color again.

"No, no, it's only a formality."

"The victim died right on top of the Swilling graves," Gretchen said. "We were hoping to learn who else was going to be buried in that plot."

"Didn't she crawl for a ways and collapse there? If that's the case, then those people buried beneath her wouldn't have anything to do with her murder anyway," Anne said. "We don't even know why she was in the cemetery after dark. Was she meeting someone? Was she with somebody? What if she had a partner, and they were robbing a grave?"

"Robbing a grave?" Gretchen stopped reading the historical document over Anne's shoulder. "Does that happen often?"

"You never know what a coffin might contain," Anne said. "Gold, jewelry. Thieves even sell body parts."

Gretchen thought Anne's theory a bit far-fetched. Gretchen hadn't seen a shovel or other tools the night the body was found. If Allison Thomasia had been trying to exhume a corpse, she would've had to have been digging with her bare hands, certainly no match for the desert rock under which the coffin lay.

Bonnie, however, was buying into her friend's grave-robbing idea. "Really? I never thought of that. Wow. I'll have to pass that one on to Matty."

Matty. Okay, now it was sounding like chalk on a blackboard or like a dentist's drill in action.

"So there's no way of learning anything about the Swilling graves?" Gretchen reached for the folder. Sure enough, no other documents were inside.

"Those grave sites have been around for a long time," Anne said. "Clients these days might talk to us about their plans for interment. You know, they might say, sure let's get a plot with enough room in case the kids want to be buried with us. You know, they like to plan into the future, just in case."

Everyone nodded.

"But they don't put that part of their plan in writing. John Swilling apparently purchased space for four coffins. That's the extent of what we'll ever know."

They were driving back to the street when Gretchen returned to wondering if the grave had any possible significance. "What if Allison crawled over to that particular grave for a reason? What if that was a clue?"

"She was trying to escape," April said. "It was random that she happened to die on that particular grave. Where she died doesn't mean anything."

"I'm with Gretchen on this one," Nina said.

Gretchen stopped the car beside Nina's car. Tutu glared at her from the backseat.

"Allison Thomasia left a clue that will lead to her killer," she said. "I'm sure of it."

145

18

Gretchen arrived home physically and mentally drained of energy. Nimrod had fallen asleep inside her purse on the way, exhausted from his fun time at doggy day care. The almost full-grown black fur ball was only the size of a stuffed animal and weighed about the same amount, next to nothing. She gently laid the pup on the sofa, poured a glass of red wine, and made a beeline for a lounge chair near the pool, where she wasted no time kicking off her shoes.

The sun was setting behind Camelback Mountain in a giant blaze of orange when Caroline joined her, favorite scotch cocktail in hand.

The moment should have been perfect, with Wobbles purring away under Gretchen's massaging hand. But the sky wasn't dark enough yet to mask the way her mother sat down gingerly next to her. Caroline turned her entire body stiffly to set down the cocktail. Gretchen smelled the minty odor of a muscle ointment.

"What happened to you?" she said. "What's wrong with your neck?"

"I had a car accident today, but I'm fine now. I took two pain pills and the Bengay is working."

"You look like you're in pain. Did you see a doctor?"

"Not yet. Maybe tomorrow, if it gets worse." Caroline rubbed the back of her neck. "If that's the extent of my injuries, I consider myself very lucky."

"Let's hear it. The whole story."

Gretchen felt her stomach churning as Caroline gave her the details of the accident.

"I assumed you had a fender bender," Gretchen said, horrified. "This is terrible. You crawled out of your car after rolling over and then attempted to assist a dying woman?"

"I couldn't believe I was alive."

"You might have been killed." Gretchen felt tears welling up. She felt scared, relieved, and angry at the same time. "Injured bodies everywhere, including yours, one person dead? And you didn't think about calling your own daughter?"

"Everything happened so quickly and others needed my help. I simply reacted. Afterward, I realized that I wanted you to hear the details from me and not before you could see with your own eyes that I was perfectly fine."

"You aren't fine."

"Please."

"You should have called."

"Really, Gretchen, I don't know what you want from me."

"You know what I want? I want my mother to stop thinking she's invincible." Gretchen found herself on her feet, tears flowing freely. "I want her, just once, to reach out to me for help. I want my mother to say she needs me as much as I need her."

"I've had to depend on myself for so long. This is all new, having you living with me."

The two women came together, hugging, crying, apologizing. "If you'd known about it you would have come there, seen the destruction, and it would have started all over again. I was only trying to protect you from more nightmares," Caroline said. "I didn't want that to happen again."

What her mother said was true. Still, they'd been through these same arguments before. "You hurt me the most when you keep things from me," Gretchen said. "When you don't include me in your life.

This is the same issue we had during your chemo."

Caroline took Gretchen's hands in her own and squeezed. "We still have a lot to learn about each other."

Gretchen sniffed. "We have some catching up to do," she agreed. "We spent too many precious years disagreeing."

She was grateful that they had worked out their differences. She'd witnessed too much hostility between other mothers and daughters instead of love and friendship.

"Cancer," Caroline said. "The disease that I thought would take my life away brought me a gift beyond anything I could have imagined. It gave back *our* life."

"We have to stick close together. We're all we have."

While Gretchen blew her nose, she caught sight of her aunt, standing behind them, a camera slung over her shoulder. "What about me?" Nina said, coming closer. "Don't I count in the equation?"

"Of course you do," Caroline said, redirecting her next hug to include her sister. "We're three of the toughest, smartest women in Phoenix."

"Good genes count for a lot of it," Nina said, taking a good look at them before frowning. "What's with you two? You both look a mess. Have you been crying?"

Gretchen shook her head. "A little, but we couldn't be happier at the moment."

After Caroline repeated her experience for Nina, mother, daughter, and aunt had another good cry.

"I love fuzzy moments," Nina said, blowing her nose into a tissue as the threesome walked into the house. "But it's officially nighttime, and I have an important mission to carry out. Care to come along?"

"Sure," Gretchen said, feeling closer to her family than ever before. Why did most special moments like this come only after near disaster?

"Don't you want to know what the mission entails before you sign up?" Caroline asked.

"Nope, I'm in. As long as it's family, you need only ask. What about you?"

"Okay, then, I'm in, too."

"Are you sure you're up to going out?" Gretchen asked her mother. "You've had a really bad day."

"I need to get my mind off the accident. My sister's always a great distraction."

Nina rummaged through the hall closet. "Caroline," she said, "where do you keep your walkie-talkies?"

"Now I'm curious," her sister said.

"What's this mission we're on?"

"We're going to the museum," Nina replied. "To gather indisputable evidence to support my claim. A disembodied soul lives in the house." She patted the camera case hanging against her side. "And we are going to prove it."

19

Antique cloth doll bodies were usually homemade. Every household had a sewing machine and a woman who knew how to use it. Creating a cloth body was a simple task. Fabrics included muslin, pink sateen, felt, and printed cloth. Before polyester, bodies were stuffed with straw or excelsior, a strawlike material made from fine wood strips. Cloth dolls and bodies are still popular today. Patterns and fabrics can be found at doll shows, doll shops, and at online doll stores.

— From *World of Dolls* by Caroline Birch

Be careful of what you wish for, Gretchen thought.

She'd made a wish and it had come true. Hadn't she wanted to work in the museum or join Nina in her ghost hunt instead of directing the play? Here she was, at the museum, working on a ghost project. But she wasn't sure she wanted it any longer.

"John and Emma Swilling had one child, a girl named Flora," Nina said while Gretchen unlocked the door to the home they were converting into a museum. "Emma died giving birth, as we thought. John raised his daughter alone. After he died, Flora, who must have been in her midtwenties by then, kept the house, moving her own family into it in the fifties and raising two children of her own, Richard and Rachel."

Gretchen turned on an entry light. Learning the names of the house's former inhabitants made them come alive for her. What these walls could tell her if they could talk!

"How do you know so many details?" Caroline asked her sister.

"It was amazingly easy, considering how hard it's been to find out who the latest owner is. I called the historical society. They dug through the records and gave me the information over the phone. I called as soon as we left the cemetery."

"Cemetery?" Caroline said, bringing up the rear, shutting the door behind them and rubbing her neck.

"Eternal View," Nina said.

Caroline glanced at Gretchen. "Why would you go there?"

Gretchen turned on another overhead

light. "It's a long story," she said. "April promised Bonnie I'd take them to the murder sight if Bonnie could make it through her lines without messing up. And she pulled it off."

"She'll tell Matt about the outing," her mother said. "How will he feel about you and his mother following his case?"

"She promised not to." At least she was hanging out with his mother. Matt should appreciate that.

Caroline rolled her eyes. "Good luck."

"Tell Caroline about the grave site," Nina said, plopping a tote bag on the counter.

"We located the cemetery plot where the couple who built this house — John and Emma Swilling — are buried."

"And you'll never guess the rest," Nina said, unable to resist taking over the story.

"I'm too tired and achy to guess," Caroline said.

"It's right where Allison Thomasia's body was found, right on top of John and Emma's graves."

Caroline was quiet while she processed the news. "That's not good," she said. "If Allison's murder is connected in any way to the past owners of this house —"

Gretchen cut her off, suddenly worried that her mother would want to halt work at the museum. "Maybe it has nothing to do with the Swillings. Just a creepy co-incidence. Remember what Matt told me, that she crawled a distance before she collapsed?"

Nina was busy emptying the tote. She pulled out items and placed them on the counter: paper, pen, flashlights, extra batteries. "Gretchen doesn't *really* think it was a coincidence that the murdered woman was found on that grave site."

"I don't either," Caroline said. The Birch women, in spite of their differences, had a few shared beliefs, one being that inter-related occurrences weren't coincidences. "These events align," she said firmly to Gretchen. "Therefore they are connected."

"I was only trying to eliminate possibilities," Gretchen protested.

"If the cemetery was a game board and you tossed a coin over it," her mother said, "what are the chances that the coin would fall on that particular grave?"

"Not good," Nina said. "I'd bet against it."

Her mother wouldn't let it go. "Exactly," she said.

Nina picked up a flashlight and handed it to her sister. "Gretchen had a bad reading, yet she refuses to redirect. Therefore, we must make friends with the house ghost," Nina said. "The spirit might decide to help us. But we can't make contact if you two keep talking."

She handed a flashlight to Gretchen, then distributed walkie-talkies. "First we need to establish rules and duties."

"Have you ever done a ghosting before?" Gretchen asked. She felt excited but scared, too. She wasn't exactly sure that she believed in ghosts, but she preferred to err on the cautious side since she was in a dark house. If this ghost existed, should she be stalking it?

"Stop with the lights," Nina hissed when Gretchen turned on yet another light. Nina followed behind her, turning them off until Gretchen could see only the narrow beams of flashlights and ghastly facial shadows.

"Who is the ghost?" Caroline asked Nina. "Emma?"

In shadow, Nina's teeth appeared long and pointy like a vampire's. "Flora," she said without a bit of doubt. Her teeth seemed to stretch out even longer.

Gretchen had heard stories of vampire ghosts. Didn't they attack people and leave visible bites on their victims' necks?

"Let's get started," Caroline said.

Gretchen felt the hairs on her own neck

stand at attention.

"Our mission is to locate the ghost," Nina said. "And to find out what it wants and how we can help it accomplish its goal." She spent several minutes going through the procedure. They would stay close enough to hear each other and make individual observations, which they would compare later.

"Why the walkie-talkies," Gretchen asked, "if we're staying together?"

"In case."

"In case what?"

Nina didn't acknowledge her. "No detail is too small to log," she said instead. "Caroline, you're the official note taker, and I'll snap photos with my digital camera."

"What's my job?" Gretchen asked. "Screaming in horror?"

"You *do* look a little pale. Want to wait outside?"

Gretchen shook her head.

"If the apparition starts speaking to us, I'm out of this building." Her mother was beaming her light along the walls, illuminating doll displays, which morphed into horror dolls.

Gretchen was having serious second thoughts. One wrong sound and she'd beat her mother to the door.

Nina snapped her fingers. "That's what I forgot. I knew there was something. I forgot an audio recorder." Nina produced a heavy sigh of regret.

"Please, let's get started," Gretchen pleaded.

"The first thing we want to do is walk around so the spirit can feel our presence."

After a pass through the lower rooms without anything unusual occurring, they gathered at the circular staircase. Gretchen shone her light up but saw only the empty steps.

"Everybody calm and relaxed?" Nina asked.

"Sure," Gretchen lied.

Caroline nodded.

"Here we go."

They slowly climbed the stairs to the second floor, guided by the flashlights' beams. Nina puttered with her camera, taking pictures in the low light. Pictures of nothing, as far as Gretchen could tell.

They entered the storage room where Nina had first encountered her ghost. The doll travel trunk was lying open where they had left it.

Gretchen moved closer and shined her light toward it, aiming the beam directly at one travel sticker, then moving it to another, forgetting briefly about the ghost mission. Vintage stickers, faded with age, represented places Gretchen had dreamed of visiting. Cairo, London, Rome, Zimbabwe, Jericho. How romantic it must be to visit such exotic, historical cities. Especially for a young girl in the 1920s. Had Flora, her doll, and its trunk really been to all these places? Or did someone bring back the stickers for her?

Gretchen was fascinated with the little girl from the photograph, but she was completely mesmerized by the doll and its wooden trunk. Her imagination soared every time she thought of the travel stickers.

"Come on, Gretchen," Nina said, bringing her back to the moment. "We'll walk slowly through the second-floor rooms. I'll take a few pictures here and there if I have an overwhelming sense of otherworldly motion, then we'll use this room as a base for the rest of the night."

"The rest of the night?" What was Nina thinking?

"This is a mission," Nina said. "Not a lark."

They wandered through the dark house, staying close to each other. Floorboards squeaked underfoot. Shadows swirled just outside their beams of light, forming into nocturnal creatures — bats, wolves, clawed animals. Gretchen was getting edgier by the second.

When she found herself lagging behind and alone in one of the rooms, she almost panicked. That's when she decided to get a better grip on her runaway emotions. She wasn't going to let a ghost reduce her to a babbling ball of blubber. Even if this house contained an authentic spirit, what could it do to her? It had no substance. It couldn't pick up a vase and break it over her head.

She was in a large room, obviously the master bedroom at one time. A triple armoire with a beveled mirror loomed directly ahead, taking up most of the space on the wall. On her left was a king-size bed with a heavy wood frame. The mattress was protected with a dustcover. Beneath her feet was a faded Persian rug.

Gretchen peered out a set of French doors that led to the balcony overlooking the street. The ground seemed far below.

Two beams of light in the hallway assured her that Nina and Caroline were right outside. Nina's husky voice floated on the air, speaking to her mother. Another assurance that she wasn't really alone.

With a rush of nervous excitement, Gretchen realized that she *did* believe in ghosts. Why else would she feel this frightened by the prospect? Could she communicate with it?

Gretchen focused on reaching out to the apparition.

If you exist, let me feel your presence.

She listened.

Nothing.

She had conveyed doubt with her thoughts. No ifs.

Let me feel your presence.

Gretchen waited.

Nothing.

Come on. Help me out. Show yourself.

She strained to hear sound. Was there a chill in the air? She'd heard about cold spots.

Silence.

Then a sound.

A noise, like a mouse. An old house like this could have nests of them. Rats, even. Gretchen hated insects and rodents, and Arizona had especially nasty ones, poisonous things with stingers and teeth. And pack rats.

The sound again, coming from over by the wall near the armoire.

She shined her beam of light directly into

the mirror. Her reflection was distorted. She looked pale, as Nina had said. Ready to flee. At least nothing stood behind her. Wouldn't that be frightening? To look in the mirror and see something not quite human behind her?

She opened the armoire doors and peered inside, finding nothing but emptiness and a faint smell of cedar.

"There you are," Nina said from right behind her. Gretchen gave in to her fears and let out a scream.

"Shhh," her aunt scolded. "You'll frighten the spirit."

Her mother stood next to Nina.

"You scared me almost to death!" Gretchen's heart pounded at full throttle.

"We came to find you." Nina was admiring the armoire. "Antique and in perfect condition. Some of the really old ones had secret compartments built into them."

"To hide an illicit lover?" Gretchen's petrified imagination was going strong tonight.

"Exactly. Let's check it out."

"I was over by the door when I heard a sound from this direction," Gretchen said. "It must have been a mouse running along the wall behind the armoire."

"I'll take a look," Caroline said.

Gretchen stepped inside the armoire and

tapped the back wall of the enormous walk-in wardrobe. Her curiosity over the possibility of a secret place was stronger than her fear. Besides, she wasn't alone anymore. She tapped the back panel again. "It sounds hollow, doesn't it?"

"Do it one more time." Nina came closer and put her ear against the panel. Gretchen tapped with her knuckles again, staring at her aunt, waiting for her opinion. Nina's eyes grew wide and she nodded.

"No sign of rodent droppings back there," Caroline said, coming around. "I'll call an exterminator tomorrow to be on the safe side."

"Come inside," Nina called out. "Gretchen's found a real honest-to-goodness secret room."

"How does the door open up?" Gretchen ran her hand over the wood, feeling for a latch or release.

"How would I know?" Nina answered. "I've never been inside one before. But hurry. Maybe it leads into the secret world of Narnia."

Gretchen couldn't help chuckling. "Why am I not surprised that you believe in fantasy worlds?" she said.

Her fingers felt something, a patch of felt, followed by the cold touch of metal. She felt it give and heard the lock release. The secret door moved ever so slightly, allowing her to get her fingers between it and the wall of the armoire.

"Ready for another universe, Nina?"

The secret door swung open. Gretchen backed up, trying to remember where she'd left her flashlight. She bumped into Nina, who moved sideways and swung her own flashlight beam into the gaping cavern of darkness they had uncovered. Her light flicked along the top of the armoire compartment then swept lower along the rich wood panel. Nina worked the light downward until it lit up something near the floor.

Gretchen felt the room spin.

Nina gasped and dropped the flashlight. Her aunt screamed.

Caroline grabbed at Gretchen's arm, trying to pull her out of the armoire.

She felt paralyzed, too shocked to move, riveted in place.

The skeletal remains of a human being were crumpled on the floor of the secret compartment.

Gretchen turned and ran with her mother and her aunt, but not before she'd seen the rest.

On the wardrobe's floor, beside the flesh-less bones, lay a small cloth body.

The doll's head was nowhere in sight.
Neither was the skeleton's.

20

He gazes curiously up the street, not that he can see the house from where he stands. He'd have to walk two blocks, then over one more if he wants to stand right in front of it.

His cherry pipe tobacco, the first bowl of the day, catches the flame from the match-stick. Smoke swirls upward on this gray morning, the first overcast sky in weeks. *Let it rain for a change, really come down in buckets.* He likes when the earth can't take the load and water runs in streams, flooding streets. Weather reporters in Phoenix have a mundane job. The same old, same old. Pollen counts aren't interesting for long. But rain, that's something to start a conversation.

Traffic — cars and pedestrians — hurries along. Already, early this morning, he has waved to some, called out to others, listened patiently while neighbors griped about this and that, pollution, smog, neighborhood pets, you name it.

All the while his thoughts bubble like a shaken can of soda, ready to explode. Especially now, with what he's just heard.

"Mr. B.," she says, calling him back from wherever his mind has wandered. "Want one?" Cramming Dunkin' Donuts into her piehole. Offering friendship. He waves it away without transferring his eyes from up the street. Nice try, but no thanks.

He hears a growl from inside a bag on her shoulder. Ratlike thing with beady eyes stares out at him. Growls again. They exchange glares. The dog looks away first.

She's finished with the tale, but he has questions. "Skeleton in the closet, you say? Imagine that." Everybody has 'em, only this isn't what she means. These are real bones. He wonders what they look like. "Anybody get a picture?"

A vigorous shake from her, whole body a big negative. "No," she says. "My friend? You know the one who dresses to match her dog? She had a camera, but she didn't pull herself together in time after the shock. It isn't every day you find a skeleton."

"Too bad. Convenient that she had a camera with her, though."

"They were trying to get photographs of a

ghost." She has crumbs on her lower lip. Brushes them away. "Instead they found a dead body. The place is haunted, you know?"

"I can see why."

What's her name again? Starts with an A. *After a month. August? April? That's it.* "You sure have the details, April." She's been spewing them at him, along with donut crumbs, one after another, like she knows what she's talking about. Wasn't even there. If he hadn't volunteered the use of his building for their event, he'd miss out on all this action. Living right upstairs helps, too, makes him feel part of things.

"They found a headless doll body in the closet, too, with the headless skeleton."

"How old do you think the bones are? Did anyone say?" The house has been vacant for what? A decade? Two? What a perfect place to stash a body. In a house nobody wants.

April chews a chunk of donut.

"Could be only a few months, I think," she says, like she knows her corpse decomposition facts.

April bounces away from the street corner and disappears inside the banquet hall. Pretty soon more of them will show up. He's still exchanging greetings when the shakes start. Like ground tremors along a fault line, his body begins to tremble and all the self-will in the world can't control it.

A group of women in the cast walk toward him, crossing the street against the light, oblivious to traffic. A car honks and they step it up. One of them looks directly at him, right into his eyes.

He's almost sick on the sidewalk.

When will she stop tormenting him?

Every last one of them looks exactly like her.

21

Gretchen's hiking boots dug into the red rocks of Camelback Mountain. She'd learned the hard way that early morning climbs were less dangerous than those made later in the day. As an expert climber, she wasn't worried about proper dress and ways to prevent dehydration. It was the creatures of the desert that bothered her the most. One too many encounters with rattlesnakes and poisonous bugs and she'd rapidly adapted to this exotic land.

The colder the temperature, the better. Not only did she have the popular mountain all to herself, without the influx of tourists and sightseers, but the rattlers were paralyzed by the cool air. Later in the day when the temperature rose, they would be lying on the rocks, sunning themselves. That is, if the sun managed to come out today.

The snakes could appear deceptively immobile, but if warm enough to respond, they could strike like a bolt of lightning.

She shuddered at the thought of thick-skinned, deadly reptiles as she reached the summit and greeted the day. Clouds hovered over her head, giving her the impression she could reach out and touch them. She wore a lightweight waterproof jacket just in case the angrier clouds in the distance reached her before she descended.

How did so many species survive in this hostile environment? Squirrels, birds of every kind, coyotes, bobcats, jackrabbits, wild pigs, all seemed comfortable and at home in the desert.

Gretchen sat and breathed in the fresh air, absorbing the quiet.

Then she climbed back down to the halfway point where an enormous boulder overlooked the city.

Matt was already waiting for her with travel mugs.

"Coffee?" He flashed the smile that had charmed her from the very moment she met him. And he wore the Chrome cologne that she loved so much.

She took the cup he offered and sat down on the boulder beside him.

"You look tired," she said.

"I have to work twenty-four hours a day to keep you out of trouble. Every time I arrive at a crime scene, there you are."

"Are you blaming me for all your problems?"

"Absolutely. But you're worth keeping in spite of the extra effort."

"Thanks."

They watched the Phoenix morning unfold below them and sipped coffee. Their relationship had reached a new level. They could be in each other's company without feeling like they had to talk every minute. Gretchen found it comforting.

She also felt a drop of water.

"It's starting to rain," Matt observed, but he didn't move from beside her.

"You're in the right field of work, Sherlock," Gretchen said, teasing, "But you still haven't learned how to dress to climb mountains. Where's your rain gear?"

Matt wore khaki shorts, a T-shirt, and sandals. "Rain gear in Phoenix?" he said. "We rarely need foul-weather gear."

"Right." Gretchen raised her face into the soft rain. "Have you found out anything about the skeleton?"

"The victim was a woman, probably about sixty years old. Dental records aren't going to be helpful since we don't have a head to work with, which also rules out our ability to forensically reconstruct the victim's facial features. Identifying the remains is going to be tricky. Our team worked through the night querying missing person databases and lining up forensics experts. The department doesn't have its own internal resources to handle the complexity of identifying the corpse without requesting additional assistance. What we really need first is a forensic anthropologist to date the remains."

"Sounds more complicated than I imagined," Gretchen said.

"The days of pounding the pavement for information are almost over. I spend most of my time at a keyboard. It's raining harder by the way."

Gretchen didn't move. This moment alone with him on the mountain was too precious to give up willingly. "Finding the skeletal remains of a human didn't really bother me as much as I thought it would. I've seen enough cadavers in textbooks, and I took anatomy in college, so I can even identify most of the bones in a human body."

"The missing head did it, right?"

Gretchen snuggled a little closer on the boulder. "The lack of a head, yes. And the headless doll body disturbed me as much as the actual headless skeleton."

She shivered. "It has to be Flora Swilling's body. Did you see the photograph of the girl holding a doll? It's the same cloth doll body. I'm sure of it."

"It could be, but we can't work from intuition like you do. I have to prove it with concrete facts. Flora Swilling married a man named Berringer. The husband died in the sixties of heart failure. I went through old missing person reports and found something interesting: In 1981, almost twenty years after her husband died, Flora Berringer disappeared. She was never heard from again."

Gretchen jumped up, excited. Nina had been right all along about the identification of their ghost. "You know we've found her!"

"We still need to make a proper identification, but for now, yes, I think you stumbled across what's left of Flora Berringer."

Gretchen felt as though she'd accomplished something big, something really worthwhile. She'd put together one more piece of a puzzle, as grisly as it was. Now the police would study Flora's history, search her background, and catch her killer after all these years.

"I want to help," Gretchen said as they started down the mountain. "I felt a connection to her from the moment I saw that old photograph."

"Now you sound like your aunt."

"If what I saw last night is all that remains

of that woman, I want to help catch the person responsible."

"That's my job."

"We can solve a cold case together."

"Oh, wouldn't that be fun."

"I knew that's what you'd say."

They had reached the trailhead. Matt's car was the only one in the parking area. They ducked into it just as the sky gave way. Rain beat on the windshield. Matt didn't make any attempt to start the car.

"Are you keeping quiet about the words on the headstone?" Gretchen asked.

"Yes, didn't Caroline tell you?"

"No, she must have forgotten."

So her mother wouldn't have told anyone. And Gretchen hadn't, which meant that the note on her windshield hadn't been left as a bad practical joke because no one knew about it.

"About the museum, Gretchen. You can't go back to it," Matt said.

"Of course I can."

"Let me rephrase that. The house has been officially sealed until we go through every box in the place and I'm satisfied that there's nothing left to find."

"When will you be finished?"

"In a few days. We're going to move quickly on this one. In the meantime, please be careful. Stay close to your family. Stay out of dark places. Make sure you're locked in securely at night."

There the warnings were again. All the rules that women were forced to live by. What must it be like to be a man, to be able to live without all the fear?

"I mean it, Gretchen," Matt said. "Put the project on hold. Stay home and work on your business."

He'd never leave her alone if he knew about the note. He'd only worry more. And what could he do about it? But she had to tell him.

Matt reached into the backseat. "I almost forgot. I fished this out of your mother's car before it was towed. You'll give it to her?"

Gretchen took the shopping bag and peeked inside. She withdrew a white plastic bag and started to open it.

"Whoa," Matt said. "You aren't going to open that, are you? What if it's, you know?"

"Oh, right." Gretchen put the plastic bag back inside. "Doll stuff." He wouldn't like that.

"So," she said after a moment, "we aren't going to be partners?"

Matt grinned and reached for her. "It depends on what kind of partners you're suggesting."

She had no intention of sitting on the sidelines like a good little cheerleader, but the man was irresistible!

A few minutes later, the car's windows were completely steamed over. And the nasty note was the last thing on Gretchen's mind.

22

Chatty Cathy was one of the most popular dolls of the sixties, coming in a close second after Barbie. Both were produced by Mattel. Chatty Cathy, who was twenty inches tall and composed of vinyl, was soon followed by Chatty Baby, Tiny Chatty Baby, and several other offshoots designed to be nurtured by eager children. Chatty Cathy's innovation was that she could "speak." Her early phrases included "Please play with me" and "Please brush my hair." With her protruding little tummy and slightly bucked teeth, Chatty Cathy was the typical, lovable child of her time.

— From *World of Dolls* by Caroline Birch

Gretchen, Caroline, and Nina crowded around the computer in the doll repair studio. Doll parts were sorted neatly inside stacked white bins, each labeled with their contents. The "basket cases," those dolls needing extra attention, were wrapped and placed carefully in bins near the worktable. Projects with approaching deadlines were also placed close to the workstations.

"See it!" Nina leaned toward the computer screen and pointed excitedly with a long, red fingernail. "It's an orb!"

"It's a smudge on the lens," Caroline said.

"It's our ghost," Nina insisted, clicking her nail on the screen.

Gretchen leaned forward and squinted at the monitor. What had she expected to find? The smoky outline of a human body? All she saw was a spot.

"Ghosts can appear as mist or sparkles," Nina said. "Orbs are most common. I'd stake my future on it: that glowing circular object is an orb."

"You're sure it isn't dirt on the lens?" Gretchen was doubtful.

Nina picked up her camera and presented the lens side to her sister and to Gretchen. "Not a single speck. It's as clean as Nimrod's teeth."

Gretchen laughed. "That clean?"

"I didn't tell you I had all the pooches' teeth cleaned. Nimrod, where are you?" Nina, decked out in black mourning as she decided was fitting after the discovery in the armoire, called out to the puppy.

Gretchen heard her tiny poodle running through the house. He barreled into the workshop, his little black ears flapping. Nimrod almost overran the spot where Nina wanted him to perform. He skidded to a stop and waited impatiently for the next command.

"Smile," Nina said to him.

Nimrod pulled back his lips, exposing his teeth and producing more of a grimace than a grin.

"My," Caroline said, laughing. "Those are clean teeth."

"Take a bow, Nimrod," Nina said using her training voice.

The poodle tipped his head in a perfect bow.

Gretchen saw a transaction between the trainer and the puppy, a treat passed so discreetly that a casual observer would have missed it.

Everyone clapped. Tutu watched aloofly from afar, miffed that she wasn't the center of attention.

Caroline held the copy of the old sepia photograph. It was the first time she had seen it.

"I'm amazed," she said, "that you found this picture."

"It's what started us on the path," Nina

said. "Otherwise we wouldn't have recognized the doll body."

"Oh my gosh!" Caroline said. "I completely forgot. I found a metal doll head in one of the boxes and had it in my car when I crashed. Matt pulled out the things from my car."

"Oh yes, he gave them to me to return. I didn't know what was inside," Gretchen said, digging under her workstation and handing the shopping bag to Caroline.

"It might be the metal head in the picture." She pulled out the white plastic bag and showed the doll head to Gretchen and Nina.

"That's it!" Gretchen said. The head wasn't in its original condition, but she could tell that it was the same or at least an exact replica. In the photograph, only shades of brown were visible, but the actual doll head had yellow painted hair and faded red lips. "Now, Nina, you can reunite the head with the body. If the police ever release it to you."

"Doubtful," Caroline said. "They'll want it for evidence."

Nina took the head and concentrated. "I'm not getting anything useful from it," she said. "Not one single message."

"It's been packed away for a long time,"

Gretchen said to ease her aunt's psychic growing pains.

"That must be it," Nina said, brightening. "Originally, I thought we had to reconnect the doll with its owner, but . . ."

Nina let the sentence die. Gretchen knew the rest. Now Nina thought the ghost was waiting for its own head.

"She helped us, you know," Nina said instead. "She made the noise that led you to the armoire. She wanted us to open it."

"Or," Caroline said, "it came from a mouse."

"No one ever believes me."

"I'd like to look through the rest of these digital images," Gretchen said, ignoring Nina's pout.

"Please do," Nina said. "We're off to plan the menu with the caterer, and I'm going to do a little window-shopping."

After they left, Gretchen remained at the computer.

She had done her ghostly research throughout the night thanks to her inability to sleep after finding human bones in a wardrobe. There was a remarkable wealth of information available online. That was the beauty of the Internet. With the click of a mouse plus a little insomnia, anyone could become an instant expert on any subject.

Digital cameras like the one Nina used were apparently notorious for producing paranormal-like orbs, especially in low lighting as had been the case in the museum. Did that mean for certain that Nina's orb was caused by flaws within the camera? Gretchen didn't know.

Other conditions that could produce false images were overexposure or flash reflections in mirrors. Then there was the problem of lens flare. Even a camera strap could cause a white vortex to appear, leading beginners to believe they had captured more exciting images than, say, an equipment strap.

She scrolled through Web sites that claimed to offer authentic pictures of ghosts. She analyzed one photo gallery after another. Some contained orbs like Nina's. One Web site claimed orbs were fakes. Another supported them as real apparition sightings. Which to believe?

The picture in question had been taken by Nina while they were mounting the steps to the second floor. In the photo the orb floated above the steps near the landing. Gretchen recalled that all three of the women had turned on their flashlights. She hadn't gone up the steps first because she was creeped out by the thought of encountering a real ghost. She had been working on collecting her nerves and was chastising herself for being afraid.

Caroline hadn't gone first, either, now that she thought about it.

Nina had.

Details were coming back to Gretchen. Her aunt had stopped midway up the stairs and snapped the first picture of the night. Before that, she had asked Gretchen and her mother to turn off their flashlights. The unexplained circle of light that Nina had captured couldn't be attributed to reflective surfaces. There hadn't been any lights il-luminated for this particular photograph.

Gretchen continued slowly through all the pictures that Nina had downloaded to the computer. She saw herself in some of them, eyes a little too wide, skin pale and promi-nent in the darkness around her, lips pressed tightly together.

She'd really been afraid.

The remaining pictures didn't produce evidence to support an apparition. They didn't eliminate it either. Every picture had mysterious shadows that could be explained away by camera glitches, lack of proper lighting, or an inexperienced photographer.

Gretchen gave up the computer search to tackle the work her mother had left on her workbench. Caroline was organized to a fault, unlike Gretchen, who tended toward extreme clutter. When they began working together, that had been their biggest problem — how to accommodate their different working styles. The only solution had been two workstations and her mother's strict orders for Gretchen to stay away from her space.

Gretchen picked up one of the dolls that she planned to repair and read the note next to it. It was a Chatty Cathy, and her mother had managed to make the doll speak again but hadn't had time to repair the pencil-post bed that came with it or to stitch up rips in the pajamas it wore.

Gretchen's job was easy. Her mother had done the hard part, making the silent doll talk.

The Chatty Cathy had side-glancing eyes, dark freckles, and buckteeth. Gretchen tugged the pull string and the doll spoke. "I love you," it said. She lifted the doll's pajama top and examined its back. There was the mark — copyright date of 1960 and the name of the doll, *Chatty Cathy.*

Running a finger over the raised mark reminded her of words written in the color of blood on the tombstone.

The dead woman hadn't been small,

around Gretchen's own height of five eight and with a normal weight, not thin, not heavy. How much bigger and stronger than Allison would her attacker have had to be? For sure, a man would have the force necessary, although a woman might have done the horrible deed with a heavy weapon and the advantage of surprise.

While preparing the materials she needed to repair Chatty Cathy's accessories, Gretchen's eyes swept past the metal head. They would have to tell Matt about it, give it up to the investigation.

Dolls should be about love, and cherishing the things that were important. Not cold-blooded murder.

To reaffirm that, Gretchen pulled on the string.

"I love you," Chatty Cathy said.

23

"April, you're a natural people person," Gretchen said, amazed at the progress on the stage. She sat beside her friend, watching the rehearsal. "You could find a position in management or in human resources. The curtain for *Ding Dong Dead* is going to go up as planned. Last week I didn't think it was possible. I'd almost given up hope."

"Did you really have doubts?" Her friend had her feet propped up on the director's table, her lap piled with pink fabric. April was sewing and directing at the same time.

"Doubts? Yes." Gretchen laughed. "When I was in charge? You bet."

"Any more news about the skeleton in the museum?" April said quietly, so as not to disturb the actors. "That sounds like a good name for a movie, doesn't it? *The Skeleton in the Museum.*"

"More like *Horror in the Closet.*" Gretchen told her what they had discovered — about the orb that Nina insisted was a ghostly spirit, about what Matt had said concerning the time required to identify the remains, and that Flora Swilling had disappeared almost thirty years ago.

April whistled at that last piece of news. "I bet she was murdered and stuffed in the closet. No wonder her ghost is haunting the place. Nina thought the most important thing was to reunite the doll with its owner, and she was close. She didn't even know about the missing human head when she said that."

The stage became noticeably quiet as the cast members dropped lines and listened to them instead. "Did they find the skeleton's skull?" Bonnie said. Standing next to the six-foot Barbie, she looked like a mustached dwarf.

"Not that I've heard," Gretchen said. Bonnie would be on the phone at the first opportunity, pumping her son for information, which was perfectly fine with Gretchen. "If you hear anything, let us know."

Bonnie wouldn't ever keep good gossip to herself. "I will," she said.

"We have the metal doll head at home," Gretchen said, going on to relate the events that led up to finding the head inside Caroline's shopping bag.

"Caroline had it all this time and didn't realize it?" Julie said.

"She's been preoccupied with her work and the accident," April said. "Can we see it?"

"I should turn it over to the police," Gretchen said. "In case it's important."

"It's time," April called, putting down thread and needle and swinging her feet off the desk. "Let's try it from the top with all the bells and whistles."

Jerome walked past and acknowledged Gretchen with a stiff nod. He adjusted a light along the stage, realigning its angle. Then he flipped off the overhead lights from a switch by the entrance, casting the room into total blackness.

"Lights, camera, action," April called. The stage lights popped on, and the mystery play began with the ringing of a doorbell.

For almost an hour, Gretchen sat transfixed, laughing at the antics of the characters. Her mother should write more plays. This one was going to be a hit. Caroline's script was perfect for the luncheon — a campy, funny mystery with a surprise twist at the end.

When the women on stage got to the part where they were considering what to do with philandering Craig's body, she saw a stab of light, and Mr. B., the owner of the building, took a seat behind them. Again, she thought of his generosity. They should do something special for him.

When the rehearsal was over, Gretchen noticed that she'd missed several calls on her cell phone, all from her mother. She hadn't heard the rings over the sounds coming from the stage. So many calls from the same person suggested urgency. She promptly called back.

"I'm at This Great Coffee Place," Caroline said. "You need to hurry over here. Don't bring anyone with you."

"Are you all right?"

"Just come. Now."

The coffee shop was crowded with after-lunch coffee drinkers getting their last shot of afternoon caffeine. Caroline sat at a table near the door next to a man wearing dark sunglasses and an Arizona Cardinals ball cap pulled low over his forehead.

"Get a coffee," Caroline said. "Then join us."

While Gretchen waited in line, greeting some of the regulars, she kept glancing at the guy sitting at the table. He had both hands cupped around his coffee as though he was cold and was trying to keep warm.

He glanced nervously toward the door every few seconds. Caroline kept up a steady stream of conversation while he listened. Several times, Caroline rubbed her neck, an indication that it still bothered her. Gretchen wondered if she'd made a doctor's appointment.

Gretchen's turn came. She ordered a latte. Coffee in hand, she went to the table and sat down.

"I'd like to introduce you," her mother said in a hushed tone, "to Andy Thomasia."

The man watched her face carefully as though he expected a negative reaction from her. Gretchen masked her surprise at meeting the dead woman's husband. "Hi," was all she could manage.

"Relax, Andy." Caroline covered his cupped hands with her own. "She's not going to do anything to hurt you. You can trust her." Then to Gretchen she said, "Right before my car accident I was rushing home to meet a very demanding customer who refused to wait his turn to see me. I found out a little while ago who that customer really was."

"I couldn't give my real name," he said. "I was afraid you wouldn't see me."

"Never, Andy."

"When you didn't show up, I thought you

had blown me off."

Gretchen noticed that her mother hadn't removed her hands. They still cupped his. He hadn't moved either.

"Where's Nina?" Gretchen hadn't seen her aunt's car outside. "Weren't you with her?"

"Andy followed us to the caterer's and approached me before we went inside. Nina offered to handle the menu selections to give us time to catch up."

"I'm in serious trouble," he said. "And I'm asking your mother for help. No, I'm begging for help."

Caroline removed her hands from his. "Tell Gretchen what you told me."

"Allison and I were separated, but we were talking about getting back together," he said. "She wanted to come to Phoenix and asked me if I wanted to join her. Of course I did! I was madly in love with her. I'd jump at any opportunity to spend time with her. That's all I wanted, to be with her." His voice broke and he paused to collect himself.

Gretchen looked away, feeling some of his pain. She'd lost her father, had almost lost her mother, and that had hurt immensely. But to lose a loved one to a senseless act of violence was unimaginable.

"When she didn't come back to the hotel," he continued, "I thought that she might have changed her mind, flown back to LA without telling me. That wasn't her style, but still, I thought that's what happened. The next morning while I was packing, I saw the news. A dead woman in a cemetery. No name. What if that woman was Allison?"

"That's when Andy went to the police," Caroline said.

"They treated me like their prime suspect after I identified her body. God, I can't go through this again." He hung his head.

"Let me explain the rest," Caroline said, taking up his story. "The police told him about the words on the gravestone and about the fantasy doll. Andy, of course, recognized her doll and also felt that it was further evidence that the authorities would use against him. He had remained in his room the night she disappeared, so he didn't have anyone to vouch for his whereabouts."

Convenient, Gretchen thought.

"Allison was studying her family history," Caroline continued. "It sounds to me, from what Andy shared, that she had become obsessed with tracing her family tree as far back as she could. She had located relatives across the country, shared her findings with other family members who were as interested as she was, and visited genealogy databases online."

"Last year she flew to New York specifically to visit Ellis Island," Andy said. "Through all this research she discovered that she had relatives who'd lived in Phoenix, so she decided to come here and learn what she could."

"Which is why she was in the cemetery," Gretchen said. "How did she get there? Do you know?"

"The police said that a cab driver let her out at the cemetery entrance with the understanding that he would return in an hour. He came back and waited fifteen minutes for her to show. When she didn't, he drove off."

"Was she meeting someone?" Gretchen asked.

"If she was, she didn't tell me," he said. "I wish I'd paid more attention to what she was doing, but I wasn't very interested in family trees. I could have cared less that she was researching second or third cousins."

Gretchen looked at her mother. "Flora Swilling," she said.

"Yes!" Andy said. "That's one of the names she mentioned. How did you know?"

"It's complicated," Caroline said.

"Oh God, I can't believe she's gone."

Andy's sunglasses were hiding more than his identity. He seemed distraught over Allison's murder to the point of near collapse. Or else he was a very good actor. Gretchen saw a tear slide down the side of his face.

Caroline looked around the coffee shop, furtive and worried. Gretchen thought they were acting suspiciously guilty of something and would call attention to themselves if they kept it up. But no one seemed to notice but her.

"You two need to appear just slightly less flipped out," Gretchen suggested.

Caroline had her hands over Andy's again. What was going on with those two? "They allowed Andy to go back to the hotel late last night," she said. "But . . ."

It was the "but" part that Gretchen found the most disturbing.

After returning to the hotel, Andy hadn't gone back to his room. "I couldn't bear to stay in the room we'd shared. I stayed in the lobby all night. I found a small alcove where I could be alone, and I stared out the window the entire night."

"Andy was there," Caroline said, "when two squad cars pulled up outside the hotel and approached the desk clerk."

"I heard my name, they headed for the

elevator, and I walked out on the street and kept going. I have to find Allison's killer before they catch up with me," Andy said. "Because every clue they have points right at me."

"Words on a gravestone implicate you?" Gretchen couldn't see how.

"You didn't see how they treated me."

"We have to help him hide," Caroline said.

Just great.

"I'm sure that if you turn yourself in," Gretchen said, "and if you are completely truthful, nothing will happen to you. The police will believe you."

"No," Caroline said. "They most certainly will not. Innocent people are convicted of crimes they didn't commit all the time. Don't you watch the news? Gretchen, we already know much of what happened. We were at the cemetery, along with Nacho and Daisy. They must know something that would help Andy."

Gretchen put her hands over her ears. "No! I don't want to hear any of this. I'm dating a cop! I can't do this. Aiding and abetting is a crime!"

But she knew that she would help, if for no other reason than because her mother had asked her to. Caroline believed in her old friend's innocence, and she was clearly going to help him whether or not Gretchen went along with their plan.

"Give us a few days," her mother appealed to her. "We'll find out what we can in the next three days. In the meantime, we'll see that Andy is taken care of."

"Caroline, this means so much to me," Andy said.

Gretchen groaned. "I can't ruin my relationship with Matt."

"You won't. If, after three days, we don't find anything to prove Andy's innocence or someone else's guilt, he'll turn himself in. Right, Andy? Do you accept those terms?"

Andy nodded. "I don't know how to repay you."

Repay us with your innocence, Gretchen thought.

"What do you say, Gretchen?" her mother asked. "Are you willing to give it a try? To give it three days?"

"Two days." She heard the words coming out of her mouth and couldn't stop them. "Two days of investigating. That's it."

"I knew you'd help," Caroline said. "We'll come back and pick up Andy here at the coffee shop around dusk. Can you stay out of sight until then?" she asked Andy.

"Sure. I've been doing a pretty good job of hiding until now." He downed the rest of his coffee and slipped out the door.

Gretchen watched him through the window until he was out of sight.

Had Andy murdered Allison? What if she had tried to leave him again and he'd killed her in a jealous rage?

Gretchen turned from the window to find her mother had been doing the same thing, watching the man disappear.

How could they be certain that Andy Thomasia was innocent of murder?

Gretchen felt chilled, and it had nothing to do with ghosts or cold spots.

24

"If you and I are going to pull this off," Caroline said from the passenger seat in Gretchen's car, "I have to come clean."

"Okay?"

Gretchen didn't want to hear more bad news. She'd had an epiphany. She wasn't the problem. Her family was. Caroline and Nina were like trouble magnets, drawing Gretchen in against her will, making her a magnet, too. All she wanted was to put on a fundraiser, decorate a doll museum, and finish lassoing her hot man.

Why couldn't they leave her alone? Now she was up to her neck in murders, bones, and hauntings, doing everything possible to destroy the fledgling relationship with Matt Albright.

"Someone in a white van tried to hurt me," Caroline said. "It wasn't driver's error that made me lose control of my car. Another driver rammed into the side of my car twice. The first time I was able to correct my direction and escape injury. The second time the driver was much more determined and I was forced into oncoming traffic."

Gretchen slowed and pulled over to the side of the street. She put the car in park. Information was coming at her too fast and none of it was good news.

Silence hung heavy inside the car as Caroline let Gretchen absorb what she had learned. Finally, Gretchen said, "Then the driver was trying to kill you."

"I'm not sure I'd go that far." Caroline saw Gretchen's incredulous stare. "All right. It's possible, yes, that the driver intended to kill me."

"He didn't count on your amazing resilience."

"It was dumb luck that I survived."

"Someone *was* killed, though. That van driver obviously didn't care how many innocent people were killed. That's unbelievably ruthless." Gretchen was horrified at what had occurred. "Why would anyone want to kill you?"

"Why would someone leave a threatening note on your windshield?"

"How do you know about that?"

"April mentioned it. She thought that it was a suggestion for a new title for the play.

She knew I'd be interested." Caroline narrowed her eyes, in mother-bear mode. "Come on, Gretchen, after a murder in a cemetery with those exact words written on a tombstone and a skeleton in a house we happen to be converting into a doll museum, do you really think *Die, Dolly, Die* could be something that innocent?"

"I wanted to block it out," she admitted. "I really wanted to believe it was a bad joke."

"You didn't want to face the truth."

"And what is the truth?"

Caroline didn't answer. Gretchen pondered the possibilities. They all led back to Allison's death in the cemetery and the bones in the museum. "Up until this point in time," Gretchen said, "we worked on the luncheon without anyone threatening us or trying to kill us."

"But after Allison was murdered, someone attempted to kill me and you found the note," her mother said.

"Someone wants us to do what? Abandon the show? Close the museum?" They weren't dealing with idle threats. They were targets. "We're in the way?"

"What's changed?"

"You began working in the house," Gretchen said.

201

"And you were at the murder scene."

"We're the only ones with keys to the museum. Is that important?"

"I don't know."

"Now what?"

"More bad news, I'm afraid. The reason I didn't want to leave the coffee shop with Andy is because we're being followed."

Gretchen stared at passing traffic, first ahead through the windshield, then in the rearview mirror. Flickers of panic shot through her. Was someone following them this very minute, parked close by with a scoped rifle?

"Are you sure?" Gretchen asked. Her Birch imagination was out of control.

Caroline laughed.

"What's funny about our situation?"

"I'm pretty sure Matt Albright's behind the tail."

"What?"

"He's having us watched. See, there goes his goon."

A squad car passed at a turtle's pace. The driver craned to get a good look at them.

"He's so obvious," Gretchen said. "How did I miss him? How long has he been behind us?"

"I'm not sure. I admire Matt for wanting to protect us, but how can we help Andy if

202

we're under police surveillance?"

"I can lose him."

Gretchen pulled back into traffic as soon as she saw the police car park up the block. She made a U-turn in heavy traffic, jamming on the gas. Caroline let out a surprised squeal. Several horns blared. And they were off.

"He's turning around," Caroline called. "He has his lights on."

Gretchen took a corner, then another.

"We've lost him," her mother said.

Gretchen turned one corner after another until she was satisfied that they weren't being followed. The only option left for the cop would be to wait at the banquet hall or their home and hope to pick them up at one of their known haunts. With the museum closed to them and April handling the show, they could easily change their patterns.

"Have you considered the possibility that Andy did kill his wife?"

"Yes, it crossed my mind, but I rejected it the moment I saw him again. Andy wouldn't harm anyone for any reason."

"How can you be that sure? I don't share your confidence. He doesn't have an alibi, and he admits that the relationship with his wife was tenuous. Not very reassuring."

Gretchen's argument sounded logical, even

to her troubled ears. "So you once had a casual friendship with Allison and Andy Thomasia. That doesn't mean you have to harbor the man from criminal charges."

"Gretchen, calm down. I can explain."

"This better be really good, because I'm jeopardizing my relationship with Matt because of your blind faith in a man you haven't seen for years."

"I should have told you much earlier that Andy and I were more than friends. We were high school sweethearts. He was my first love. Our senior year we went in different directions, grew apart, but we kept in touch occasionally."

Gretchen tried to imagine Andy and her mother together. It wasn't a pleasant thought. She'd never imagined her mother with any man other than her father. "What about Dad?"

"That was long before I knew your father. Come on, don't you remember your first boyfriend?"

She *did* remember her first love. She thought of him occasionally and wondered where he was and what he was doing. He held a special place in her heart and always would. But that didn't mean she would protect him if he was accused of murder.

"Don't you understand how I feel?" Caroline asked. "Even a little?"

"Knowing helps."

But not much.

In her opinion, anyone was capable of murder given the right circumstances. Andy Thomasia hadn't convinced her otherwise. Neither had her mother.

25

Terry Vascar scans a stack of messages that came in through police dispatch while he was out. He kicks back, feet crossed on his desk. As a member of the Violent Crime Bureau, he collaborates closely with Phoenix PD Laboratory Services, Missing Persons Detail, and the medical examiner, among others.

Today he is reviewing events with Matt Albright. They have collaborated on cases ever since graduating together from the academy.

Their division has more cases to solve than they can handle. The department is short on trained personnel, and they try to prioritize the cases the best that they can. A recent murder takes precedence over old bones in an armoire. Not to mean they are being ignored. Only that Matt will have to count on others to assist with some of it.

That's where he comes in.

Terry will let Matt know what he finds.

"Allison Thomasia is my most important concern right now," Matt says. "Along with substantiating evidence to support the investigation."

"Andy Thomasia is on the run," Terry says. "It's only a matter of time before he surfaces. A man like that can't last for long as a fugitive."

Matt rubs his face with both hands, as if attempting to rub away exhaustion. "The suspect and the victim were estranged," he says, "but according to the husband, they were reconciling."

Rule number one, learned in the first week of the criminal justice program: assume everyone is lying.

"The victim could have changed her mind," Terry says. "She might have decided to move forward with the divorce. Rage, jealousy, unrequited love. All powerful motives for murder."

Matt nods, and Terry thinks of his friend's problems, the former wife's cunning, her manipulative tactics, would have been enough to make a weaker man consider murder.

Matt's lucky to be rid of her. Finally.

"The suspect didn't have an alibi," Matt says.

"Tough for him."

Usually a suspect can come up with at least one witness, even if the timing isn't perfect. But this guy doesn't have a single one, not a hotel desk clerk or a bartender who can establish an out for him. Never a good sign.

And the suspect was certainly strong enough to crush Allison Thomasia's skull, given the right weapon.

Andy Thomasia could have had all three — motive, opportunity, and means.

"If only they would locate the murder weapon," Terry says.

"They will."

Police have searched the hotel room. Nothing there, but Terry isn't surprised.

"Blunt force trauma to the back of the head," Matt says. "Lacerations suggesting an object such as a hammer. But also sharp cuts, three deep incisional wounds. I called the ME. Not a claw hammer, she says. It isn't sharp enough."

Terry and Matt go through the different types — sledge, club, ball, brick.

Matt likes the brick hammer idea. "It's designed for breaking bricks," he explains. "It has a blunt end, but it also has a sharp end. It's a possibility as a murder weapon."

"Is your suspect a bricklayer?" Terry asks.

"No. He's a mechanical engineer."

"A handyman type?"

"No idea. Can you put someone on it and start checking hardware stores?"

"At your service," Terry says.

The Thomasia woman had crawled from one gravestone to another. The perpetrator had attempted to drag her away. Why had he stopped? Fear of discovery? More likely the trail of blood that followed behind the victim canceled out his efforts to move her to a different grave site.

The sharp blows that finished her off were delivered at the second headstone.

No defensive marks on the victim's knuckles or under her fingernails. The attack was unexpected, but the perpetrator wasn't. Allison knew her killer.

Matt's phone rings.

"They found Andy Thomasia's California driver's license," he says when he disconnects, already rising from his chair.

"Where?"

"Under a bush at the entrance to Eternal View Cemetery."

"That takes care of it then."

"Maybe."

Rule number two: assume the possibility that evidence has been planted.

"Something is out of whack," Matt says.

He doesn't stick around to explain, but
Terry agrees.

26

Andy Thomasia was waiting near the coffee shop at the arranged time. He rode in the backseat while he listened carefully to the impromptu plan that Caroline and Gretchen had implemented on his behalf. The original idea to stash him away in their home was no longer feasible, given the police protection that seemed to be in place.

Two days, Gretchen reminded the former sweethearts. The deadline was Sunday at three in the afternoon. If they didn't have a killer in their sights with enough information to go to the police, Andy would turn himself in.

"Why was Allison's doll at the cemetery?" he wanted to know.

"That's what I want to ask you," Caroline said.

"I have no idea, although she did bring a few dolls along on the trip to give as gifts if she found any relatives. It makes me think she *was* meeting someone."

"Are you sure you were staying with Allison?" Gretchen said, dispersing with social etiquette and cutting right to the chase. "You don't have a clue what her plans were. You can't tell us who she met, where she went, or what she was doing."

"Research, I told you. Genealogy study of her family history."

"You must have more than that," Caroline said. "A name, an address, something to help us?"

"I don't care about things like who her third cousin twice removed might be. Come on, give me a break. All those charts and tree branches, who cares?"

Charts? Gretchen thought. *Of course!*

Gretchen almost slammed into the car ahead of her when it stopped at a light. She looked at Caroline, then glanced quickly back at Andy. "Were these charts computerized?" she asked.

"She had a printout in her purse," Andy said. "But the police told me that she didn't have her purse when they found her. She used a computer program to record her genealogy research, and while we were in Phoenix, she carried a notebook. That's gone, too. It would have been inside her purse."

"Did she bring her laptop?"

Andy shook his head.

"Can we access her home computer records?"

"Without going back to LA, I don't see how."

Gretchen stopped the car in front of a central Phoenix soup kitchen. Daisy had been quick to agree to their plan. Nacho, on the other hand, had reservations but had acquiesced with a little prompting from his fiancée.

"We're leaving you with some friends," Caroline explained to Andy. "Trust them. They won't turn you in. What they will do is give you different clothes to wear and show you how to fit in. Follow their example. Watch how they act and follow suit. No one will look for you here. You'll be in good hands."

Andy nodded.

Gretchen gave her mother's old friend a hard look to convey her feelings of distrust. "We won't make contact with you until we have something to go on. Word will come to you through those who are helping."

"I understand."

While Caroline was inside getting Andy settled in his new environment with their homeless friends, Gretchen contemplated her next move. She couldn't access Allison Thomasia's computer, but she knew who could.

"Detective Albright," she said when he answered his phone. "I have information for you."

"Ms. Birch. So pleased to hear from you."

"Were you worried?"

"Should I be?"

The man liked to answer her questions with his own. She knew he had to be concerned, because their tail would have informed him that he'd lost the Birch car. Too bad.

"You sound excited," he said with a playful amusement in his tone she could tell was forced. "What is this intriguing information? A new doll collection purchased by your lovely mother that will make you a rich woman? A newly opened restaurant to which you are about to invite me?"

He was going to be so angry with her in a few more minutes. Gretchen almost hung up.

"We have a bad connection," she said. "I'll call you back."

"I can hear you perfectly fine."

Great.

"What I have to say is important."

"I'm sure it is."

"Allison Thomasia was related to our skeleton. I mean to the Swilling family. She was in Phoenix researching her family tree."

"Yes. I know." A harder tone.

Jeez.

"Check her computer. She kept computerized records of her findings. You might find something useful in them."

Heavy, heavy sigh on the other end. "I've already done that. Where are you?"

"Uh, running errands."

"You're hiding from me, aren't you?"

"Of course not. I can't believe you think that. Why would I hide?"

She could have told him that the Birch women were busy trying to keep from getting killed and that to accomplish that goal they were aiding and abetting his primary suspect.

He'd read her rights to her if she'd said that.

"Are you any closer to finding out who tried to kill my mother?"

"She told you about that?"

"Of course."

"We're making progress. Where are you?"

"Don't worry about me. Get to work and catch bad guys."

"We're doing the best we can."

Not good enough!

"I appreciate your concern over my safety," Gretchen said. "The police protection was thoughtful and sweet, but we need to do this our way, not yours."

"Who's 'we'?"

"My mother's with me."

Since he was already worked up, Gretchen decided to tell him about the note on her windshield.

"I need to see it," he said.

"It's missing."

"I'm putting out an APB." He was really, really mad, if she was any judge of male voice tones. "And how do you know about the victim's computerized family history? What do you think you're doing outrunning an officer of the law, Gretchen?"

She ended the call.

Was he serious about the APB? Could he have her picked up? She doubted it. What was he going to do? Have her arrested every time she did something he didn't approve of?

Gretchen sensed a glitch in their previously harmonic relationship. They had had another disagreement.

Hopefully, it wouldn't be their last.

27

Caroline and Gretchen spent the next hour parked in the crowded lot of the Biltmore Fashion Park making phone calls and warning their other club friends to be on the alert. No one knew why Caroline and Gretchen had been targeted, but all the Phoenix Dollers agreed that the Birch women must have crossed someone, someway, somehow.

Gretchen and Caroline had been the driving force in negotiating the terms of the agreement regarding the museum; they had been singled out to represent the club by the attorney and had handled most of the transaction. They were also the only members with keys to the house, a stipulation required by their benefactor.

The other club members debated whether they too were in danger; it was a possibility they couldn't ignore.

April had a theory.

"The most active members of the doll club are in big trouble," she said when she answered her cell and learned of the day's events. She considered herself in that group, along with Bonnie and Julie. The women would spend the night with friends and stay close together during rehearsals. They were armed with lipstick-size pepper spray, gifts from Nina to all the club members last holiday season.

"It's the pattern of threes," April said. "Everything, including murder, comes in threes. Sets. For example, we eat three meals a day."

Gretchen had heard this before.

"Three cheers," April continued. "More sets of three — Hip, hip, hooray. Small, medium, and large. Three again. And then abbreviations. ABC, AAA, PTA, TNT, VIP. Before, during, and after. More threes."

April was building steam. "How about jokes? The minister, priest, and rabbi. The blonde, brunette, and redhead. Tom, Dick, and Harry. All threes."

"Third time's the charm," Gretchen added when April paused for breath. "Gotta go."

Nina offered to make sure Wobbles was well fed. She'd also pick up Nimrod from their house immediately and keep him with her. Nina, in case she was also on their adversary's bad side, had her own safety plan.

"I'm staying with Brandon for a few days," she said coyly, turning the situation to her advantage. "It'll give me a chance to see if he's strong relationship material. No sense getting too involved if we aren't cohabitatively compatible."

Gretchen hadn't thought of asking Matt for help. Instead of arguing with him should she have moved in under his protection?

Not that he'd offered.

Not that she would have taken him up on it. She wasn't the type of woman to play the helpless card. If they were going to make it for the long term, he needed to understand that she wasn't going to walk two steps behind him.

Gretchen felt better after talking to her friends. For now, everyone was safely off the streets and holed up in various hideouts.

Thinking of being holed up in hideouts reminded Gretchen of her father's sister, her aunt, Gertie Johnson, who ran her own investigative business in the backwoods of Michigan's Upper Peninsula. She'd given Gretchen advice in the past that had helped her get out of some tight places.

It was too bad that Gertie and Nina didn't get along. The two women weren't related by blood, but Gretchen's aunts were very much alike — eccentric, opinionated, and stubborn — which was a major contributing factor in their inability to see life through the same type of lenses.

Gretchen could use some of her Midwest aunt's homespun solutions. If only she didn't live across the country.

While Caroline sat next to her in the car talking to Bonnie on her cell, Gretchen called Aunt Gertie. She answered right away.

"How are things in the wild Southwest?" her aunt said.

It took a long time to relate the entire situation from the very beginning, but Gertie was a good listener, rarely interrupting, although she produced several vocal sounds, ranging from snorts to tongue clicks.

Caroline hung up from her call and leaned back in the seat with her eyes closed as Gretchen continued on.

"Whowee," Gertie said at the end of the story. "That's quite a tale. Do you want my opinion?"

"I would appreciate it more than you could possibly imagine. I'm putting you on speaker phone, if that's all right. Then Mom can hear what you have to say."

"Hi, Caroline," Gertie said. "You're in a

fine mess."

"You could call it that."

"Here's what you need to do. Ready?"

"Ready," Gretchen said.

"Find out as much about the Swilling family as you can, and I don't mean the family tree branch like who's related to who. You need the more personal stuff, like where are those kids? Find out what happened to Flora's son and daughter. What are their names?"

"Richard and Rachel."

"Them. Find out if they reported their mother missing."

"I'm sure the police are following up on all those connections," Caroline added.

Another of Gertie's tongue noises. "In case you've forgotten, I have a son who is a sheriff, and I can't count on him for much in the way of law enforcement. Your cops in Phoenix might be fancier than ours with more resources, but the first thing you have to decide, if you want to live, is that you can't count on anybody else to handle it for you. You want a job done right, do it yourself."

"Gotcha," Gretchen said. "Go on."

"Get that new owner's name, the one who owns the museum house."

"How, though?" Gretchen said. "The attorney is adamant about protecting his client."

Caroline leaned closer to the speaker. "I tried to get the information through city hall records. The property is part of a trust. The terms of the trust aren't public record."

"Then rough up the lawyer. He'll spill."

Gretchen loved the way her aunt spoke, tough and to the point. And from what Gretchen had heard, her aunt's actions were as strong as her speech. "How are we supposed to learn about the Swilling family? They're all either dead or missing."

"You told me they owned that house for decades."

"Correct."

"Somebody must still be living in their old neighborhood, someone who would remember the family. And if there was gossip concerning them, that person would remember every last detail of any rumors, too."

"Thanks, Aunt Gert, you've been a big help."

"The only thing I'd suggest that you ignore," Gertie said, wrapping up the conversation, "is Nina's stupid idea about haunted houses and ghosts. That woman is several cards short of a full deck. Find something harmless for her to do before she hurts herself. And keep me posted."

Caroline and Gretchen had done all they could for the time being. Government buildings were closed for the weekend, making it impossible to delve into any more historical records, and their friends were on high alert.

"What about us?" Caroline said, sounding worn out. "We could go home."

"That's probably the last place that Matt will look for us," Gretchen agreed. "Or we could stay with Daisy, mingle with the invisible people."

"I'd rather not. I'm getting too old to sleep on hard ground without a pillow if I don't have to."

"And I need computer access if I'm going to track down some of the present-day Swillings. I just hope a few of Flora's family members are still alive."

They drove home without encountering any police protection officers. Gretchen drove into the garage rather than leaving her car in the carport. They left the lights off so the house would appear empty, and without another word, Gretchen went to her room and collapsed in bed.

The only thing she heard before morning was a soft and steady purring from Wobbles.

28

Five o'clock Saturday morning Gretchen poured a cup of coffee and made herself comfortable at the computer, expecting that the task would take a long time. The first item she found in her Internet search came quicker than expected. Rachel Berringer's name was listed in the *Arizona Republic* obituaries. Two brief impersonal paragraphs to prove that Flora Swilling's daughter had once existed.

Rachel had died in March of the current year.

Gretchen learned more from what was left out than what was said. There wasn't a "survived by" list of close relatives. There wasn't any hint of the cause of death as in many obituaries where the causes were made known through requests for special donations. The obit didn't say anything about "in lieu of flowers." Rachel had died at sixty-three, hadn't taken on another last name through marriage, and had left no children. There was no mention of interment or visitation services.

That was it.

After an unsuccessful search for more information, Gretchen considered that avenue of inquiry a complete dead end. The obit didn't even tell her where Rachel had lived or died. Just because the obituary ran in the largest paper in Phoenix didn't mean Rachel Berringer had died in Arizona. She could have been a former resident. Gretchen wondered who had been responsible for placing the information in the newspaper.

The only detail of minor interest was that Rachel had died the week before that anonymous donor had offered the Phoenix Dollers the use of the Swilling family home. Had she been that donor? Or had ownership passed to another relative? And what about Richard? Was he their anonymous benefactor?

Gretchen would delve into Rachel Berringer's past after all the intrigue and drama died down, after a killer was identified. The club should make some sort of dedication to the deceased woman and to others in her family who had made contributions to the collection. They should be immortalized within the museum.

Next, she searched for Richard Berringer, keying in various combinations of last names. She got over fifty thousand hits. This one was going to be more complex. Gretchen didn't have a starting point for the brother, didn't know anything significant to narrow the search criteria.

She refined the search to Phoenix and the surrounding area. Several hours later, she still wasn't any closer to finding Richard Berringer.

He hadn't been mentioned in Rachel's obituary.

Who knows, she thought, *maybe he's dead, too.*

29

Doll repair can be likened to surgical procedures performed by medical surgeons. The best doll doctors have an array of specialized instruments and are skilled in their use. Doll doctors must be adept at putting patients back together again. In a sense, they restore life.
— From *World of Dolls* by Caroline Birch

"What are you doing here?" attorney Dean McNalty asked, looking from one woman to the other. His eyes, distorted by the lenses of his Coke-bottle glasses, appeared overly large and reptilian. He sat behind a desk of worn, marred wood, surrounded by cheap vertical file cabinets. The carpet was faded and dirty. Gretchen wouldn't have taken a seat in the old upholstered chair if someone had threatened her life.

"I'm surprised to find you in your office on Saturday," Gretchen said.

Thrilled, really!

"What do you want?"

"We'd like to take a quick peek at a file." Gretchen smiled sweetly.

"Confidential," he grunted. "We've been through this already. I have a responsibility to my clients. I wouldn't last long if I divulged personal information."

Caroline walked around behind the desk. Attorney McNalty tried to watch both women at once, but the logistics weren't working well for him. He wasn't an owl.

"We thought you might say that," Gretchen said. His eyes swung back to her. "But we have resources at our fingertips. We can convince you otherwise."

"Get out of here," he said, looking over his shoulder to see what Caroline was up to.

She casually displayed a surgical scalpel. "A tool of the trade," she said. "I use it in my workshop for repairing dolls. My particular line of work requires a razor-sharp blade and a keen eye for using it."

"What are you doing?" McNalty's voice hit a high note. He started to rise from the desk. Gretchen stepped closer, displaying her own repair tool. The attorney sat back down with a thump.

Gretchen wondered about the direction of

her moral compass. What were they doing?

"You have two choices," she said to Dean, throwing aside her doubts. "You can tell us which one of these cabinets contains a certain file. We don't have time to search through them to find it on our own. Deadlines, you know. Second choice, of course, is protect your client. Then we'll have to carve the information out of you."

McNalty's eyes grew wider, if that was possible.

"And," Caroline added, "we're very, very good at slicing."

"The file is in that one right there," he said, pointing. "Second drawer down, filed under *Swilling*."

"Stay where you are," Gretchen warned him. She opened the drawer and quickly found the file.

"The Swilling home is owned by a trust," Gretchen said to her mother, skimming through the paperwork. She glanced at McNalty. "You're the trustee?"

"You'll have to sort it out on your own," he said. "I'm not helping you."

"According to this, John Swilling established the trust upon his death. It can't be sold by any of the beneficiaries." Gretchen glared at the attorney. "This is going to take time for me to understand. Why don't you

229

make it easy?"

"That's impossible."

Caroline flashed her weapon. "We don't have time for this. Explain the document."

"Okay." McNalty held up his hands. "Back off with that thing." He adjusted his thick glasses. "You're right. The house was placed in trust with the stipulation that it would remain in the family. Until her untimely death, Rachel Berringer was the beneficiary of the trust. Although she didn't live in the house, she continued to show interest in its maintenance up until she died."

"What about her brother?" Gretchen asked.

"We weren't able to locate him in spite of our well-intentioned efforts. After a reasonable amount of time, he was declared dead in absentia."

Gretchen tossed the file on his desk. "How could he just disappear?"

"It happens all the time," McNalty said. "People want a new start, or they have a reason to want to avoid discovery. Perhaps Richard Berringer committed suicide or committed a crime under an assumed name. Mental illness might have caused him to vanish. Who knows?"

"Who is the current beneficiary of the

trust?" Caroline asked.

"I hold ownership of the trust for the benefit of the trust's beneficiaries," the attorney said. "I located a distant relative who resided outside of the state. Before I could make contact, I discovered that the next in line was actually living right here in Phoenix."

Gretchen paged through the document while McNalty was speaking. "Trudy Fernwich."

"Yes."

"Where does she live? How can we reach her?"

"That is your problem."

No address was listed on the document. "Let's go," she said to her mother, dropping the file on his desk.

Within minutes, they were out the door and on their way.

"Will he call the police?" Caroline asked.

"I don't think so," Gretchen said, hoping she was right. "All he lost was a little professional dignity. And it's his word against ours."

They had come for information, and they left with what they came for. Neither was sure what to do with it.

They knew the name of the distant cousin who was the newest beneficiary of the trust that owned the Spanish Revival house that the club was converting into a museum.

But they had never heard of her.

30

Nacho has heard the man's sob story and isn't at all moved by it. They'd spent the night inside a shed, down a dead-end alley. He isn't about to show a stranger into the home he's created under the viaduct. He built it himself out of plastic and duct tape. Gray to match the girders. Only his real friends know about his place, and he's keeping it that way.

He's not dumb.

This Andy has money in his pocket but doesn't have a bit of street smarts, waving the roll of bills around like he wants somebody to take it away from him. If Nacho hangs with this guy too long, he'll worry about his own future health.

What he'll do for his friends. And Caroline is one of the best.

Andy bought him a nice bottle, a token of his gratitude, and that counts for a lot. You don't look a gift horse in the mouth.

Nacho's getting married to the love of his life and has promised Daisy that he will dry out. Soon. He'll do it soon. She's promised to help him beat his demons, and he'll do anything for her. Right now though, he's drunk on gold-label whiskey. Johnnie Walker. Eighteen-year-old blended to be exact. He knows his liquor.

Andy's a talker, which suits Nacho. He's observing instead of participating, which is his style. Sit back, stay alert, absorb. All night, he tipped back, wetting his lips, savoring the amber liquid, watching it swirl like the gold it's named after.

Otherwise he would have been bored out of his skull, having to listen to how this guy's wife had left him and he'd been trying to get her back. How they came to Phoenix thinking the trip away from LA would be good for them, and how it wasn't.

How she had told him right before she was killed that it wasn't going to work after all.

Andy was just as drunk as Nacho, even more, slurring his words, nodding off, waking up, and continuing his boo-hoo story.

They all had it rough. Why should this guy's problems be any worse? All kinds of people have wandered through Nacho's life. Every one of them thinks they are worse off than the next guy. Like it's a big competition and being the biggest loser is some kind of win.

This blurry Saturday morning, his guest is sleeping off one big-mama hangover, while Nacho is out and about, still drunk but searching for someone.

The word's out to the other street people, along with a description of the person he wants to find: a skinny doper who works for anybody who'll hire him, no name, as in NoName. That's what they call him. Has a red pentagram tattoo on his neck, the five-pointed star inverted to point down, surrounded by a black circle.

This particular person doesn't mean anything to Nacho, but Daisy has put in a request. Gretchen and Caroline are in need of assistance. Anything he can do, he will.

Time to find the guy who shouldn't have been in the cemetery the night of the murder.

31

Gretchen looked out the window of This Great Coffee Place at the same moment that April banged her white Lincoln's bumper into a parking meter directly in front of the coffee shop. Nina jumped out of the passenger seat and said something to April. Judging from the expression on her face, she wasn't very happy with her new partner's driving skills.

At the first sign of real trouble, Bonnie had abandoned them for a weekend in Glendale with a different group of friends. Julie went off to Tucson. *Turn up the heat*, Gretchen thought, *and you find out quickly who can take it and who will abandon you for a more temperate climate.*

"Unbelievable," Caroline said when a traffic cop came into sight in time to witness April's destruction of city property. He didn't look pleased as he listened to April, who appeared to be arguing with him.

Nina pushed past April and was addressing the police officer.

"I'm only thankful," Gretchen said, ducking back from the window, "that I can't hear what Nina is saying to the cop."

"She'll get April out of it."

"Calamity Jane has an extensive driving record with the motor vehicle department. Springing her is going to be tough. April's an accident waiting to happen. Why is Nina riding with her? I thought we had agreed that we'd live longer if we didn't let her drive."

"Nina stayed with Brandon last night."

"I know."

"He decided to surprise her by tuning up her car today. She said he had it ripped apart before she woke up. By then it was too late to stop him. She griped plenty when we couldn't come and get her."

April wore a yellow pantsuit, accessorized with an orange ribbon headband tied around her head, its long showy ends trailing down her back. Nina had on a tiger-striped wrap dress and gold heels.

Gretchen rose from the table and chuckled. "I'm not sure if we should split those two up when we start canvassing or stay as far away from the peacocks as possible. I didn't think to tell them to play this low-key."

"I can't partner with Nina," Caroline said. "We'll disagree on everything and end up mad at each other."

"I'll take her. You and April work one side of the block, we'll do the other. Let's go."

Nina had finished convincing the officer that April didn't deserve a citation. Gretchen saw him walk away without writing anything.

But her aunt wasn't finished complaining to April. They arrived outside in time to hear April tell Nina to "buzz off."

The four of them walked down the street, two of them stomping a little more angrily than the others. They passed the banquet hall and went another two blocks where they turned the corner and stopped in front of World of Dolls.

Caroline spoke first. "If I didn't know differently," she said, "I'd think it's just another work day at the museum."

"It looks exactly the same," April agreed.

Nina was staring up at the second-floor windows.

"Looking for your ghost?" Gretchen said.

"She's watching," Nina said, not taking her eyes off the house. "I know she is."

"By the way," Gretchen said, only that

moment remembering all the tiny responsibilities, "where are the dogs? Day care?"

Nina gave up on window gazing. "Doggy day care is closed on the weekend. I didn't have a choice."

"They're at your house?" Gretchen could only wish. Fat chance of that.

"No. Yours," Nina answered. "They're keeping company with Wobbles."

Gretchen and Caroline groaned in duet.

The dogs were wonderfully well behaved, if Gretchen didn't count Tutu, until they got together. Then their primitive pack mentality got the better of them. The last time they were left unsupervised, the canines had run wild; the house looked like a war zone by the time Gretchen got home.

"Let's get started," Gretchen said since she couldn't do anything about the dog situation. "We're going to canvass the neighborhood. With any luck, we'll find someone who has lived in this area for a long time, long enough to know the Swilling's family history and give us some background."

Caroline handed each of them a notebook. "Jot down the addresses you visit and the results. We don't want to waste time by repeating the same houses later. Make notes if you discover anything that could be relevant."

The women teamed up under Gretchen's direction. She watched her mother and April knock at their first house before she crossed to the other side of the street with Nina.

Six homes later, after four unanswered knocks and two occupied by owners too recent to be helpful, Nina started complaining about her feet, then about the task at hand. Gretchen glanced at her aunt's gold heels but didn't say anything.

"Phoenix, in case you haven't noticed," her aunt said grumpily, "is a transient city. Everyone living in the Valley of the Sun is from someplace else these days. We're wasting our time on a wild-goose chase."

"Do you have a better idea?"

"I could be spending the day with Brandon."

"Under the hood of your car? That sounds like a good time."

"You have a point."

Nina remained on the sidewalk holding her shoes and wiggling her bare feet while Gretchen knocked on house number seven. Again, there was no response.

From what Gretchen could tell, Caroline and April were having more luck getting doors to open but the same rate of failure finding longtime residents. April called over.

"Nothing yet," she said. "We're turning the corner up ahead."

"Whose big idea was this anyway?" Nina wanted to know after putting her heels back on.

Gretchen couldn't tell Nina that she'd talked to her aunt Gertie. Something about her other aunt's name brought out the very worst in Nina. And she was crabby already. "We have to at least try," she said. "We'll finish what we started by circling the block."

"Wait," Nina screeched. "Don't tell me." Her eyes became narrow, knowing slits. "You've been taking advice from that woman again?"

Nina's intuition was sharpening, but Gretchen wished she would use it for a higher purpose than arguing with her. Why couldn't she use it to identify the killer?

"Aunt Gertie made a few suggestions," Gretchen said. "They seem reasonable."

"There isn't anything reasonable about her. She's dangerous. Practically everyone around her gets shot to death."

Gretchen couldn't help letting out a small chortle. Nina was close to the mark. Aunt Gertie didn't always think before she acted, sometimes creating more problems than she started with. But she always solved her cases. For her, the end justified the means.

"You're exaggerating, Nina," she said.

As usual.

They stood in front of a house set slightly farther back from the street than the other homes. Gretchen thought it had an unoccupied look to it. Not exactly that its exterior hadn't been maintained, though it appeared neglected when compared to the others. She walked past it.

"Where are you going?" Nina asked from the sidewalk that led to the house. "What's wrong with this one?"

"No one lives here." Gretchen stopped and turned around.

"Really," Nina said.

"I don't think so, but I suppose we should make sure."

Nina had another "incoming message" expression on her face when Gretchen passed her and started up the walkway. "Someone's inside," her aunt informed her.

Gretchen was on the porch about to ring the doorbell.

"Don't!" Nina shouted. "I have a bad feeling!"

What was the matter with Nina? At this rate, they'd be on this block for the rest of the day. Gretchen pressed the button and heard the chime inside the house. "What's wrong with you?" she asked her aunt.

Before Nina could reply, the door creaked open.

A large woman loomed in the doorway, staring at Gretchen.

"I'm searching for information on a neighborhood family," Gretchen said.

"Come in," she said. "We've been waiting for you."

32

Collectors are experiencing renewed interest in metal-head dolls. Since it is difficult to find an undamaged metal head, the following instructions are useful for restoration. Remove all the original paint with an oven cleaner. Have your local car accessory dealer mix a flesh-colored spray paint in a satin finish. Apply two coats, allowing time to dry between coats. Use acrylic paints and an airbrush to add cheek blush. Artist's brushes work well when painting facial features. Finally, lightly apply antiquing patina through an airbrush at a distance to give your metal head an authentic old look.

Metal heads are forgiving. If you make a mistake, simply start over.

— From *World of Dolls* by Caroline Birch

Terry Vascar and Matt Albright watch the start of the excavation while the noon sun beats down on their unprotected heads. Standing beside them is John Meyer, a forensic anthropologist, and Frances Castillo, medical examiner, professionals considered the best in their respective fields. They are also good friends, having shared more than a few drinks over discussions concerning unusual cases.

Terry swipes at a trickle of sweat running along the side of his face.

He feels adrenaline shooting through his veins and a growing impatience with the time it has taken to arrange the equipment and workers. Matt looks as frustrated as he is.

All worth it.

He fervently hopes.

Ground-penetrating radar, aka GPR, has detected an object under the surface of the Swilling's family plot. That in itself isn't notable, considering that this is a cemetery, after all. What makes this discovery unique, though, is that this object is near the foot of a buried coffin. It should be a patch of desert dirt through and through. No record exists inside the cemetery office of anything beneath this piece of ground. In fact, no records are available for this entire section of the cemetery.

Terry and Matt have finished watching the

technician radiate high frequency waves into the ground. They have received lessons in electromagnetic energy and geophysics when variations are reflected in the return signal, more technical jargon than either needs or wants.

Their main focus is on the final results from the radar.

The buried object.

A man in grass-stained pants hurries toward them. The caretaker.

"See right here," he says, pointing, tapping the earth with the toe of his boot. "The ground's been disturbed. I knew I should report it after what happened the other night. The dead woman and all."

This red Arizonian dirt is brighter than it would be if it had remained untouched. Sun and air pales exposed earth. Someone dug in this spot recently. And their equipment proves that a metal object is below. Could it be the murder weapon?

"Careful," Matt warns. "We don't want it damaged."

Per Matt's orders, the team is digging wider and deeper than the GPR expert recommended. Better safe. Whoever placed the object at the base of the grave site wanted to keep it from discovery.

The cemetery is busy with visitors today,

a typical Saturday. Those tending the graves are fulfilling their obligations to the deceased. A few curious spectators have stopped to watch them work.

"Got something," one of the men says, digging his shovel into the mound of earth and bending down.

They all gather closer, anxiously waiting as precautions are taken, police procedures are followed to a T, not a single deviation permissible under the detectives' watchful eyes.

Terry stares at what the digger has unearthed. It's a human skull.

John and Frances go to work on it while the diggers continue to seek the metal object.

"Violent death," John the forensic pathologist mutters, confirming Terry's suspicions.

"Any guesses?" Matt asks the ME.

"It's possible," Frances says. "I won't know until I get it in and compare it to the other victim, but it could be from the skeleton, and killed by the same murder weapon." She studies the cranial material. Even Terry can see where the blows have crushed the skull.

John rises from his task. "Skull hasn't been in this shallow grave for long," he says.

Terry nods his understanding. Matt

glances at him. "We found somebody's buried treasure," he says.

"Some treasure," Terry replies.

Frances had already informed them that the remains in the armoire had been in that location for years. "We can assume that she was killed in the house," she had said. "And hidden inside the wardrobe."

"It appears possible," Frances says now, cautiously, always hesitant to make statements prior to full investigation, "that we've got a match."

"So," Matt says, "at some point recently the killer moved the head, hid it here."

A van filled with a television news crew pulls up as close as possible considering the number of visitors' cars parked in the area.

"Trouble," Terry says.

"Like bloodhounds," Matt agrees. "If they make a connection between the two murders, they'll be screaming serial killer." He stalks off in their direction. Terry is confident that the team of media clowns won't get near them.

What kind of person did this? A sociopath, Terry thinks. Superficially, sociopaths are charming, pleasant, easy to like. But covertly they are hostile and cunning. Lies roll easily, smoothly enough to even pass lie detector tests. Terry sifts through the knowledge stored in his brain. Sociopaths harbor deep-seated rage, an inability to feel remorse, a view that other people are nothing but targets.

Terry would rather deal with a rabid dog. At least he'd know what he was facing.

The news crew is setting up near their van. Matt returns to the group, stands with his back to them, concealing as much as possible from the camera lens. Terry does the same.

"There's more," a digger says, exposing a white plastic bag.

Gloves, bags, pictures. Minutes elapse before the plastic bag is opened and the contents exposed.

Not a hammer, but oddly, a metal doll's head. The head is old, with painted yellow hair and blue eyes, chipped and fading.

Before the doll's head is completely revealed, Terry senses that Matt isn't next to him any longer. He is some distance away, talking on his phone. Terry approaches, notes that his friend has lost his composure. He is pale, shaky. Terry's never seen him this way.

"They're out of town," Matt says, ending the call, his voice ragged likes he's just run a five-kilometer race in record time. "They're safe."

"Who?"

"Gretchen and her mother. I just talked to Caroline. They're not in Phoenix."

Terry's aware of Matt's feelings for Gretchen. He knows about some of their personal conflicts, about the Birch connection to this case.

"What's wrong with you?" Terry asks, seeing that his friend is extremely agitated, pacing, sweating.

"I recognize the doll's head," Matt says. "It was in Caroline's car. After the accident, I pulled it out and gave it to Gretchen. Which means that whoever buried the skull and doll head was inside the Birch house yesterday."

"Are you sure?"

But Matt isn't listening. He's making another call.

"Send a car over to the Birch house," Matt barks into the cell phone. "I want twenty-four-hour surveillance. Stop anybody going in or coming out."

Matt is on a roll now, he has his composure back, but he's reactive rather than proactive, never the best place to be. Terry doesn't like defense, preferring to play his games offensively. Matt's the same way.

"We have to step up the search for Andy Thomasia," Terry says.

Matt agrees. "We also need to find the missing son," he adds. "Richard Berringer better surface soon, either as a live body or on a death certificate."

"We'll get them."

"Damn! The nerve to break into Gretchen's home and take the head."

Terry glances toward their team. "A doll head buried in a grave and a doll body in a wardrobe inside the Swilling house. Bet they're a match."

Yes, this killer fits another classic sociopath characteristic.

They like to live on the edge.

Terry runs his eyes over the gravestones, suspicious of everyone, all the people coming and going, visiting the dead. He stares at the handful of spectators.

"If he touches her," Matt says under his breath, "I'll kill him with my bare hands."

33

Gretchen and Nina slid through the door into the dilapidated house.

"We've been waiting for you," the woman had said. What was that all about?

Nina had hung back, concerned about entering. She'd sputtered about the bad aura permeating the building, but followed Gretchen inside after calling Caroline on her cell to let her know where they were.

The other part of their team would continue with the search and meet them back at the museum in approximately one hour.

The living room smelled of talcum powder and mothballs.

"I'm Nora Wade," the woman said, showing them to a flowered sofa covered in yellowed plastic. "This is my mother, Bea."

Most of the mothball smell seemed to be coming from the old shriveled woman sitting in a matching upholstered chair in a corner of the small room. Heavy drapes on the windows were pulled shut. A lamp on an end table supplied the only light.

Gretchen gave Nora her warmest smile before she said, "Our doll club is renovating the Swilling home, and we're searching for history on the house and the Swilling family members. We are looking for neighbors who may have known them."

A knowing look passed between the other two women.

An affirmation that they knew the family? "Did you know them?"

Another look at each other before Nora nodded.

Wonderful. They'd found someone from the old days who might be able to help.

"Would you like some tea?" the mother, Bea, asked. Her voice was so low that Gretchen had to strain to hear her.

Gretchen shook her head.

"No, but thank you," Nina said.

"What did you mean," Gretchen asked, "when you said that you had been waiting for us?"

Nora sat down on the edge of the sofa close to Gretchen. The heavy fragrance of talcum powder came from her. "We weren't waiting specifically for you, but it was only a matter of time before people started wondering about that family and the house.

You couldn't have been inquiring about any other. Besides, we've seen you in the neighborhood. You're the ones who are restoring the Swilling house."

"Please tell us what you know."

As it turned out, Nora Wade's mother had lived her entire life in the home they were in at the moment. Gretchen didn't think a single piece of furniture had been replaced during all those years. And the drapes must have been drawn to keep natural light from exposing layers of grime and the sorry condition of the furnishings. Dust danced in the lamplight.

"I remember when Flora disappeared," Bea said, speaking slowly and softly. Gretchen again strained to hear. "The family had so many tragedies, one right after another. You've known families like that, I'm sure, where everything goes wrong for them."

"Yes, I have," Gretchen said.

"The family had a long history of mental issues, but Richard had the most serious of the lot. Rachel was one year younger than Richard, and he hated her from the day she was born. He was a willful, jealous child, and when Rachel was ten, he tried to smother her with a pillow."

"Shocking," Nina said.

Gretchen and Nina exchanged concerned glances. If psychic ability ran in families as Nina believed, then Gretchen had a little of her own and was feeling it now. It wasn't warm and fuzzy. She felt as cold as one of Aunt Gertie's Michigan winters, as if her veins had turned to ice and were slowly freezing her arms and legs.

"His mother stopped him in time," Nora said. "But he became more and more dangerous as he grew. Richard started along his violent path in the same way many people with mental problems begin. He was horribly cruel to animals. His poor sister would tell the most awful stories about him."

"A lot of whispering went on in the neighborhood," Bea said. "I tried to tell Flora about the danger her son posed, since we were friends, but she wouldn't listen. The entire community was afraid of him. Finally when he was a teenager, the family sent him to a special place for people like him. What a relief for the entire neighborhood's sake."

"Did he ever return?" Gretchen asked.

Bea shook her frail head. "No. Rumors came and went about what happened to him. Some said he existed in a vegetative state after a botched lobotomy. Others thought they spotted him on the streets of Phoenix periodically. I always suspected he was dead. Then that woman from California showed up here looking for Rachel and strange things began to happen."

Gretchen sat up straight. "Did you meet Allison Thomasia? Did you speak with her?"

"My mother didn't," Nora said. "But I met her while I was out on one of my daily walks. She was standing in front of the Swilling house, staring at it. I asked her if she had a special interest."

"When was this?"

"A few months ago. When was it, Mother?"

"About then."

A few months ago? Had Allison been in Phoenix all that time? Or had she made two trips?

"She was tracing her family history," Nora said. "She said she was related to the Swilling branch. I gave her as many details as I could, like I'm doing now. Recently that young woman was found dead in the cemetery."

"Yes, we know," Gretchen said. "She designed dolls."

"She had a nice doll with her. Kind of strange for my taste, but you could tell that she had talent even if it wasn't my cup of tea."

Gretchen asked Nora to describe the doll.

Flowing hair, fairy wings, ivy on the doll's leg. It was the same one found in the cemetery.

"She said she was going to give the doll to the next relative she met," Nora said. "She liked to do that, give away dolls, she said. The dear never had a chance."

Gretchen was pretty sure that Allison had found her next of kin. But the doll had been discarded along with the dollmaker's body. "Do you know why Rachel didn't live in the house anymore?"

"Too much misery," Bea said. "Flora's daughter had mental problems of her own."

"Well," Nora said, "we don't know that for a fact. But she had more than one side to her, that's for sure. Not that I'd speak ill of the dead."

"Of course not," Nina said.

Gretchen remembered Flora's metal-head doll and her travel trunk. "One more thing," she said. "I have a picture." She found it in her purse and handed it to Nora. "Flora's doll trunk fascinates me. Do you know how she got the travel stickers? Did she really visit all those wonderful places?"

Nora got up and took the picture over to her mother. "That's Flora. The memories this picture brings back!" Bea said. "Mr. Swilling, Flora's father, was an archaeologist. He traveled to foreign locations to participate in digs and always returned with stickers."

That explained the exotic locations represented by the doll trunk's stickers. Cairo, Jericho, Rome. Cities with important archaeological significance.

"Did you find Mr. Swilling's rock collection in the house?" Nora asked.

"No," Caroline said. "But we found the doll Flora is holding in the picture."

"If I were you," Nora said, "I'd stay away from anything having to do with that family. The house and the family, if anyone's left, are cursed."

"Really?" Nina said, showing more interest than previously. "A curse?"

"She meant that figuratively, Nina," Gretchen said. They didn't need a ghost *and* a curse. She shot her aunt a warning glance and projected out, *No ghost stories, please.*

It didn't matter whether or not Nina picked up the unspoken signal to refrain from telling her own ghost theory, because Nora stood up, signaling the end of their conversation.

"Go home now," Bea whispered, appearing more shrunken than ever. "You're pretty girls. You don't want to be next."

34

Gretchen and Caroline worked side by side at one of the library's computer workstations. Expanded search strings had failed to produce information on Richard Berringer.

Caroline typed in a search string. *Insane asylum patient lists.*

Thousands of pages of records came up for institutionalized patients throughout the country.

"This is going to take days," Gretchen said, scanning page after page. "And we can't be sure his records were ever computerized."

"And once we find the records, they won't give us information about the present. We still won't know where he is." Caroline rubbed her neck. "The best we can hope for is a better understanding of mental disorders, so we know what we're dealing with. Here it says that the Insane Asylum of Arizona dates back to the 1800s. Thousands of patients were committed to it against their will. But then during the human rights movement, a bill was passed. It stated that a person had to be dangerous to themselves or others to be confined."

"Before that, no one needed a reason to commit another person?"

Gretchen was shocked at the facts regarding sanatoriums, at the absence of any kind of patients' rights. She was developing a new appreciation for how much society had changed in regard to mental health laws.

Gretchen pulled up a lengthy list of patients and their diagnoses from an asylum that had been located on the East Coast. Insanity conditions, according to the charts, ranged from hallucinations to dementia, incoherency to delirium of grandeur.

"Delirium of grandeur?"

"Same as delusions of grandeur. In my day," Caroline said, as though she were an ancient artifact, "families could band together and institutionalize another family member. It was a convenient way to remove dangerous people from society, whether the threat was perceived or real. If your relatives thought that you might harm yourself or someone else, off you went. Of course, some people took advantage of the law and abused their power. Patients were sent away because they were afflicted with diseases or had certain disabilities that their families couldn't or didn't want to deal with."

"I can't imagine our society allowing that to happen," Gretchen said.

"But we did. The mentally ill could be placed in a facility and abandoned forever," Caroline said. "The laws eventually changed, thank goodness, and people could no longer be institutionalized against their will. Over time, the insane asylums closed. Many are abandoned buildings to this day."

"What happened to a released patient after the new laws were passed?" Gretchen asked.

"They rejoined society the best they could. Many were released in downtown Phoenix to fend for themselves. Social service agencies that could have rehabilitated patients for re-entry into society didn't exist. Some of the released patients' families would have taken over the responsibility of caring for them. Some must have become homeless."

Gretchen leaned back and rubbed her weary eyes. "Mentally ill patients were abandoned on the streets without professional care. One of them could have been Richard Berringer."

"That's right. Or one might have been Rachel, based on what Nora and Bea told you."

"But she's dead. We need to find out what happened to *him.*" The task was monumental. If they had weeks maybe, but they didn't.

After a few minutes of contemplating the Berringer family time lines, Gretchen opened the notebook she had carried while canvassing the Swilling neighborhood. She began drawing a simple sketch of a family tree, constructing branches and filling in dates of births, deaths, and disappearances. Information from the Swilling gravestones helped, but most of the doodles were Gretchen's assumptions.

She drew a tiny question mark next to Flora's name, then, remembering what Matt had told her, crossed it out and wrote the year the woman had vanished: 1981. "We can assume for now that she was murdered close to or on the day she disappeared," she said to Caroline, who had stopped searching to watch her daughter work.

"She disappeared in the early eighties," Caroline said. "At a time of social change, when patients in the sanatorium were being released. We don't know that Richard was still in an insane asylum when the laws changed."

"But the dates fit." Gretchen looked at

her simplistic effort at charting a family's history.

Richard Berringer, Flora's son, could be the killer. But would he have murdered his own mother? And what about Allison Thomasia? Did he kill her because she came too close to the truth behind his missing mother?

She could imagine the scenario.

The Berringer family's son Richard was mentally ill. He might have had many issues, an established pattern of violence. The family had to deal with his problems once and for all. Prison or an asylum? Which would be worse? They made a choice. He remained in a sanatorium for years. Then changes to the mental health laws put him out on the street without follow-up treatment for his condition and without a place to live.

After that, his mother disappeared.

Did he return for revenge and kill her, leaving her decaying body in the armoire?

If an enthusiastic family genealogist showed up asking questions, delving into his past, he might have arranged to meet her at the cemetery. He might have murdered her.

Everything made sense.

If Allison found Richard and told him of

her plan to search through the family's past, that meant he was near, close enough to lure Allison into the cemetery to silence her forever.

Richard might be living under an assumed name. Or he could be one of the homeless that Gretchen had seen at the rescue mission or at the soup kitchen.

Richard Berringer could be anyone.

Caroline's phone rang, interrupting Gretchen's thoughts of murder. Her mother, immersed in reading an item on the Internet, handed it to Gretchen without looking at the caller ID.

"We went to pick up the dogs from your house," Nina said. "A cop stopped us outside. Then your honey showed up."

Gretchen heard April whooping in the background. "What a man!" came through loud and clear.

"Quiet down, April," Nina said. Her aunt sounded tense. "I can't hear myself think."

"You didn't tell him where I was, did you?" Several library patrons glanced toward her. She rose from her chair and walked out into the entryway for privacy.

"No, I didn't tell him," Nina said. "But only because I promised you I wouldn't. Isn't he on the same side as we are? I don't get it."

"Someone tried to kill your sister," Gretchen said, keeping the threatening note and concerns about her own safety out of the conversation. "Matt doesn't want to give us the chance to help her. He wants to place us under lock and key. If he had his way, we'd be behind bars while he machos around."

"He's so protective, not to mention smart," her aunt said. "Let him take care of both of you. Your last reading was a bad one. You need all the help you can get, and he's one explosive package to have on your side."

"I know it sounds crazy, but I have to be my own woman." Nina wouldn't understand her inner turmoil. She needed to say it out loud, to listen to herself, determine if she was acting like a kook.

"You're still reacting to the split from that control freak," Nina said. "Matt isn't Steve."

Gretchen had allowed herself to be marginalized in the past, and it would never, ever happen again. She could and would protect herself and her mother from whatever life threw at them, which was why they were in the library at the moment.

Whether or not it made sense to others didn't matter. It was what she had to do, and her independent mother felt the same way. Together, nothing could stop them. She hoped.

"Did you get the pets?" she asked Nina.

"Matt let us take them, but Wobbles took one look at the crate I was going to put him in, and he did a disappearing act. After I looked and looked without finding him, Matt said he'd stop by frequently and take care of him."

"How is he going to get inside?" Gretchen said. "The only people with keys are you, me, and Mom. Oh no. You didn't? You gave him your key."

"He thought someone had been inside the house."

"What!"

"Matt's keeping an eye on things."

"Is anything missing?"

"Matt asked me to look around. I didn't find anything missing."

"Are you sure nothing's missing?"

"How can I be sure? Your workshop is filled with stuff. The television is still here, though."

Great.

"Matt's taking care of us."

"That's reassuring."

"He wants you to call him."

"Yes," Gretchen said. "I'm sure he does."

35

Andy Thomasia sat up from a crouched position in the backseat of Gretchen's car. Instinctively a scream of terror rose into her throat. She swallowed it down, tasting bile.

You deserve this, she thought.

She was outside the library, alone, her car parked in an isolated back corner of the lot. Her mother was inside, unaware that her daughter had even left the building. Gretchen hadn't checked the backseat. She hadn't seen him until it was too late. She was already inside the car, checking her cell phone's car charger to see if the phone had full power. Gretchen couldn't possibly have been this careless.

But she had been.

Andy wore the same dark sunglasses and Cardinals ball cap that he'd had on yesterday, but his clothes were different. They were dirty, torn, and too large for his body. Nacho had done a thorough job of turning him into a homeless person.

"I locked my car," she said. "How did you get in?" Did her voice give her away? Could he hear the fear?

Andy held up a long, narrow strip of metal. "I got in with this," he said. The tool was a lock-picking device like those cops used to open locked cars. Andy's voice was neutral, not threatening or overly aggressive. Not friendly either.

The inside of the car was stifling hot, having sat in the sun for hours. She felt a slick layer of sweat against her skin.

"Why did you break into my car?" Gretchen spoke quietly and calmly. She had more than a few questions for the murdered woman's husband. "I told you that we'd contact you."

She had a firm grip on the door handle in case she had to make a run for it. No one was around to help her.

Andy leaned forward. She didn't move. Gretchen had been wary of Andy before. Now she was downright terrified.

"I'm here because I have new information," Andy said. "I need to get it to Caroline. I hadn't expected you to come out alone."

Gretchen couldn't read him, not his voice or his expression.

"I didn't expect you either," she said, turning her body so her back was against the steering wheel, as far from him as possible. "My mother's inside the library. I'll relay the message to her."

"You don't trust me, do you?"

"Of course I do," Gretchen lied. "Otherwise I wouldn't have agreed to help you."

"I didn't kill Allison. I loved her. Even if we weren't able to work out our problems, I would have continued to support her dreams. Allison's fantasy doll line was taking off," he said. "She was starting to make money, finally breaking in. I wanted her to succeed."

"I'm sure you did." Was her tone patronizing? She hoped not. "Did Allison make an earlier trip to Arizona?"

"Yes. She was here in March, doing initial research. I wish she'd never come back here. If only I'd known."

"What did you want to tell my mother?"

Still no one passing by the car.

"Nacho made the rounds this morning looking for a guy," he said. "Apparently someone was in the cemetery the night that Allison was killed, who wasn't part of the normal homeless community. But he didn't tell the cops that."

"The street people don't like cops much,"

269

Gretchen said.

Andy nodded. "For good reason, I'm finding out."

"And this guy?"

"He's a common crook type who runs some action on the street. Nacho found him. He told Nacho he was hired to rob me."

"By whom?"

"He never met his contact."

"Convenient."

Andy nodded. "This thug was paid to pick my pocket, steal my wallet, remove the driver's license, and replace the wallet. And it had to happen on a certain day."

"What day?"

Andy looked pained. "The day Allison was murdered," he said. "The person who hired him made it very clear that I wasn't to suspect anything was missing. And it worked. The guy was smooth. I didn't notice a thing."

Gretchen watched Andy's face. Was he making this up?

"The guy would get paid double for the next part of the deal."

"Which was what?"

"He was supposed to drop my driver's license in the cemetery at a specific time. The guy ran late getting there though, so instead he threw it in a bush by the entrance when he saw the cops pull up. After that he was trapped and taken in along with all the others that were rounded up for questioning."

"So your driver's license is in the cemetery."

Andy shook his head. "The cops have it by now."

What an unbelievable story! Gretchen had to get out of the car, get away from Andy Thomasia, and run for the safety of the building.

He grabbed her shoulder. "Don't you see?" he said. "Someone planned the whole thing ahead of time. Allison's death was premeditated, not some random act of violence. And I was supposed to be arrested for her murder."

Gretchen pulled away from his grip, carefully arranging her face to convey compassion and understanding. "Then go to the guy who robbed you and make him cooperate. Turn yourself in and have him substantiate your story."

"Nacho said the guy wouldn't help me, and Nacho wouldn't give me his name. And why should the guy help me? He'd be incriminating himself."

"Andy." Gretchen had to make her move

to escape before it was too late. "How did you find us at the library so easily?" she asked. Would she have time to grab her phone from the charger? Not likely. She'd have to leave it behind.

Andy leaned back in the seat, which was what Gretchen was waiting for. "It was the strangest thing," he said. "I told Nacho that I wanted to find Caroline. Not long afterward, he gave me your location. It's like there's some kind of communication system, but I don't know how it —"

Gretchen slammed her body against the driver's door at the same time that she released the handle. The door flew open and she was out. If Andy had a weapon besides the lock pick, she hadn't seen it yet.

She broke into a run, aiming straight for the library, relieved that she didn't hear him chasing her. Every muscle in her body was taut, and she was very aware of her exposed back.

She gained the steps leading into the library. Several other patrons were also entering.

The only sound Gretchen could hear was her own ragged, frightened breath.

36

A librarian tapped Gretchen on the shoulder. "We're closing in five minutes," she said.

Late Saturday afternoon and the Birch women had nowhere to go.

Caroline had previously downplayed her old friend's actions. She'd wanted to believe in Andy's innocence; she'd known him for so long as a friend, and as more. But she reluctantly sided with Gretchen after hearing about the incident in the car.

Caroline's defense of Andy ended when she learned that his driver's license had been dropped at the murder scene. Had it happened the way he told it or had Andy lost it after killing his wife? Anything was possible. They would no longer take chances, even when dealing with old flames.

Andy now had the backing of the homeless community thanks to their foolhardy confidence in him. They would have to find

Nacho or Daisy and rectify that. Otherwise the homeless people could continue to help Andy locate them.

"Saturday night," Gretchen said. "We'll never find them."

"Let it go," Caroline said. "We don't have any proof that Andy is a murderer. Besides, we promised to give him two days. If we don't discover anything useful by then, we'll turn the entire problem over to the police along with the information we have so far."

"We can't go back to the car," Gretchen said. "He might be waiting."

"Even if he's not, Nacho and his tribal drumbeaters know what we're driving." Caroline gave her a weak smile. "I never thought I'd have to hide from Daisy and Nacho's street family."

"Or from Matt," Gretchen added. "I'd like to get my cell phone out of the car, though."

"Really, Gretchen, you're too attached to that thing. We have mine."

They called a cab and gave the driver the address of the banquet hall. On the way, they contacted Nina and April and asked them to meet them there. "Leave your cars someplace else," Gretchen advised them. "As many blocks away as you can comfortably walk. We wouldn't want anyone to pass the building and see familiar cars parked right in front of it."

Within an hour, the four women were sitting with an oversized Barbie doll on the edge of the stage, eating burgers picked up by the ever-ravenous April.

Tutu, Nimrod, and Enrico whizzed around the room, playing chase games and looking for mischief while Caroline and Gretchen brought Nina and April up-to-date.

"You need to get into witness protection," April said when they were finished.

"I don't think they have those kinds of programs anymore," Nina replied.

Gretchen addressed her aunt. "Why don't you use your psychic powers to help us out? It's worked in the past. Can't you put out a distress call?"

"Mayday, Mayday." April giggled.

"I can't perform on demand. Messages come in randomly, and they aren't one hundred percent reliable."

"Walk backward," April suggested. "I heard it helps stimulate psychics."

"The exercise isn't about walking backward. I'm supposed to *think* backward," Nina said. "And it isn't appropriate for this case."

"What if you held an object and concentrated," Caroline said. "Would that work?"

"Like what?" Nina asked, looking doubtful.

"I know," April said around a cheek filled with burger. "A piece of the skeleton would be good. Except I'm sure the police removed it from the house."

"Yuck. I'm not touching any dead person's bones."

"It should be something connected to the victims," Caroline said.

"What about the photograph?" Gretchen said, remembering that she had a copy of it in her purse.

"I held it before and didn't feel a thing." Nina drained her soda and set it down on the stage floor. "But I'm pretty sure the killer is male."

"We already suspect a man," April said. "That isn't useful information."

"What's your reason for believing it's a man, Nina?" Gretchen wanted to hear everyone's conclusions. Maybe something would jump out at them. Other than ghosts.

"I think a man killed Allison and the same man is after you, because I have trouble 'reading' men." Nina held her fingers up in quotation marks. "When we went near that neighbor's house, I got a powerful incoming message. And there was a reason for it. They knew something important, yet disturbing.

Women are easy. Men, I can't do."

"In other words," Gretchen said for clarification, which tended to be a difficult task when dealing with Nina, "when we found the bones in the wardrobe, if the corpse's killer had been a woman, you believe that you would have known that through a feeling or a message."

"Right. But I didn't, so it's a man." She glanced around the group. "I think."

Gretchen heard footsteps overhead.

"Mr. B.," April said, shifting her eyes to the ceiling.

Heavy shoes banged down the stairs from the apartment above. A moment later, Mr. B. entered the room. "Thought I heard something down here," he said. "What are you doing rehearsing on a Saturday night?"

"We're not," Caroline said. "We're just going over some of the finer points."

"Four good-looking women like you should have dates."

After a couple minutes of polite conversation he left, banging back up the steps, leaving behind the scent of cherry pipe tobacco. Gretchen sighed. Mr. B. was right. She should be out with Matt.

What was all this drama doing to their relationship?

Did they still have one?

37

The four women reflected on the stories about Flora's son Richard related to them by Nora and Bea Wade.

"Does mental disease run in families?" April asked when the story was over.

"Genes account for so much," Caroline said.

"That's right." Nina stroked Tutu from the canine's seat of power on her lap. "Look at our family. We're spiritual and we have special abilities." She glanced sharply at Gretchen. "If only we'd accept them."

Caroline, the oldest, was the most knowledgeable about psychiatric procedures practiced in the seventies and eighties.

"Shock therapy was big," she said. "And could be given against a patient's will."

"I've seen it in movies," April added. "Patients were strapped down to tables with no anesthesia and all those wires attached to their bodies. Then the seizures. I can't even think about it without feeling faint."

Caroline nodded. "Electroshock was used to treat depression."

Gretchen had done her Internet homework. "And schizophrenia."

Nina chimed in. "Anybody with emotional problems in those days was labeled schizophrenic."

"That's correct," Caroline said. "The label was overused. But as far as electroshock goes, we learned at the library that over a million people each year still receive it. Of course, now the procedure is voluntary."

"Who would do that?" April said. "How creepy."

Gretchen was overwhelmed by the amount of information they'd discovered. "I think everything we've discussed tonight should remain between us."

"What happens in the banquet hall," April said with a grin, "stays in the banquet hall."

"Seriously," Caroline said. "Very soon, we'll go to the police."

"Where do we go from here?" Nina said.

Gretchen looked over at her mother. She didn't like the plan they had concocted on the way over in the cab. It had been her mother's idea, and Gretchen couldn't really see the point, but she didn't have a better idea.

"Here's our idea," she said, jumping into what she was sure would be extremely hot water.

38

When the women leave the banquet hall, Jerome rises up from behind the stage curtain and stretches out his cramped muscles. Lucky for him, he heard them fumbling around with the lock and whispering. If they'd found him asleep in a stage chair, he'd have been screwed. In the nick of time, he took a dive behind the stage and didn't move a single muscle.

They stayed long enough to worry him, his body complaining like all get-out, but he remained in a frozen position. How much longer could he do it?

As long as it takes, he said in his head more than once.

He sure heard an earful, though. *Man! Craziness,* he thinks, *is in the eye of the beholder.* It's shifty. Who gets to decide? Other crazies?

He heard the whole thing from beginning to end, and now he's in the driver's seat again. He is back on track, just like the strip of lighting he installed over the stage.

For a time there, he'd lost their trail. But Jerome's a smart guy. He knew they'd show up at the building eventually. He's good at waiting, like when he's after a bird. Cats are the same way, although he hates cats, for what they do to birds. But he's an observer of behavior, and cats know how to get what they want.

It's only a matter of who has the most patience.

He rummages through the garbage in the break room, pulling out the burger bags and eating what he can find, pieces of bun, a little hamburger meat, bits of lettuce. Finished with the scraps, he wipes his hands on the gray overalls. He decides right on the spot that he likes to wear this one-piece outfit. The pockets are wide and deep, perfect to fit a bird inside.

Weapons and birds are his fields of expertise.

Everybody's special in some way, if you just take time to find it and accept it. You don't have any control over some things, so go with the flow, he always says, and make use of your skills.

The women left some coffee in the pot, lukewarm, but hey, beggars can't be choosers.

He pours a little for himself, using the same cup that Gretchen Birch drank from, the one with her name on it and little dolls dancing around the rim. He can smell her scent right along with the coffee smell, and it is as rich as cream.

Jerome inhales, enjoying himself immensely, satisfied with life.

He isn't in any kind of hurry.

Because he knows exactly where they are going.

39

April and Nina, along with their canine entourage that included Nimrod, would spend the night at Brandon's house. Under different circumstances, Gretchen would have found humor in the situation. Brandon Kline hadn't known what he was getting into when he began dating Nina. This family came with a lot of baggage, most of it living and breathing, and Nina was throwing all her curveballs at him at once.

Her aunt drove the few blocks to World of Dolls in silence. *Mentally exhausted like the rest of us,* Gretchen thought. *And angry.* They'd had a heated debate over the wisdom of Gretchen and Caroline's choice of accommodations and were barely speaking to each other.

Nina had continued to disagree with them even as they were leaving the banquet hall. "You're fulfilling your destiny. You can't seem to wait for your share of misery and disaster. Check into a hotel. I'll pay."

"Nina," Gretchen had replied, "we *want* to stay there, so leave it alone. Join us if you'd like."

"I'm giving up. This is so foolish," Nina had shot back. "Like one of those old slasher movies where the woman just *has* to go down into the basement, knowing that the killer is in the house. How stupid is that?"

"I love scary movies," April had said as Gretchen inserted her key into the keyhole and opened the door leading into the World of Dolls Museum.

Now, as Gretchen made her way up the spiral staircase, she wondered again what they hoped to learn from the house and its ghostly occupant. A hotel would have been simpler, safer, and less nerve-wracking. Every creak in the floorboards frightened her. The small protection she carried in the form of a lipstick-shaped cylinder of pepper spray didn't reassure her much. She wished it were a semiautomatic weapon.

Aunt Gertie, where are you when I need you?

And where was her other aunt when she needed her? It was uncharacteristic of Nina to turn down an opportunity for adventure. Nina had claimed that she refused to accompany them because of the danger of inciting wrath in a ghost whose remains had been improperly removed from its domain. "The bones might be gone from the house," she had said, "but the ghost has been left behind, and it will be angry."

"Ghosts must have their own personalities," April had said. "Like people. You can't predict their moods. You're thinking up excuses."

Gretchen silently agreed.

What Nina really wanted was to be with her man. Who could blame her?

Soon, if all went well, Gretchen would be wrapped in strong, manly arms of her own. Matt Albright would be all hers.

With her mother beside her, she paused to listen at the upstairs landing.

Not a sound.

The light of the moon had guided them through the lower level of the house, past the doll displays arranged in more easygoing days. It seemed so long ago. One of the dolls appeared to move, causing Gretchen's throat to constrict and her heart to beat wildly. Then she realized it was only a cloud passing across the moon, creating patterns of dark and light inside the old house, giving inanimate objects a sense of motion.

To make matters even more difficult, they

286

couldn't risk any artificial lighting, not so much as the smallest flashlight beam as they found their way along the upstairs hall and into the master bedroom where the armoire had revealed its long-kept secret.

"This is it then," Gretchen whispered. "We might as well get settled."

"Why are we tiptoeing and whispering?" Caroline said, whispering back.

"I don't know," Gretchen said, speaking at her normal volume but finding it shockingly loud. "If a ghost is around, it knows it has company. No amount of sneaking is going to help us hide from it. I'll be right back."

"No, we have to stay together."

"I'm only going to the next room. Relax."

Using the wall for support and guidance, Gretchen moved through the rooms and returned moments later, carrying the doll trunk.

She sat down on the bed next to her mother. "Nina's right," she said. "What do we hope to accomplish by spending the night in this creepy place?"

"We have the same stubborn streak," her mother said. "We're doing it because no one else wants us to."

Gretchen laughed. That was part of it. "We might get lucky and find another clue.

Do you really think Nina saw a ghost come from this trunk?" she asked, feeling the travel stickers beneath her fingers.

"Nina's paranormal experiences began when she was a child. At first they scared her. She told us about them, but no one in the family believed her. I pretended to. Sometimes, I really *did* believe her. She's been on target with her predictions enough times that I have to wonder if she has some special talent to see the future."

Gretchen smiled to herself. "Maybe our ghost was trapped inside the trunk for years and Nina released her."

Caroline laughed lightly.

They lay quietly for a time. Then Caroline said, "Isn't it special that we still spend quality time together at our ages?" She gave a tiny chuckle. "Mother and daughter on a sleepover."

Gretchen laughed along. "It's funny when you put it like that. A sleepover in a haunted museum. You rock as a mom, just so you know."

"Thanks. I try to keep it interesting. And speaking of interesting, you seem to be fascinated by that trunk."

"I am, though I'm not sure why."

"Go ahead and sleep. I'll take the first shift. In the morning, if our ghost hasn't given us answers to help solve Flora's or Allison's murder, we'll plan our next move. I can't believe I'm doing this. We must be awfully desperate."

Gretchen was tired. Her head throbbed, but lying down helped.

Caroline reached over and massaged Gretchen's shoulder. "You know," she said, "your father was an amateur geologist. He had an identification book and a few tools to crack rocks. Do you remember when the two of you would go out in search of fossilized stones and pore over that book?"

Gretchen stretched out. "I forgot all about that!"

She yawned and closed her eyes. A soft sound of a light breeze playing against wind chimes rode on the air. She drifted along with the melody.

The night hours passed slowly. Gretchen was restless. The house sounds were unfamiliar to her, and she had one ear tuned to every little noise.

She had finally drifted off when Caroline clutched her arm.

Gretchen's eyes flew open.

"I heard something coming from the other side of the door," her mother said, staring at the closed door. "It woke me."

"Is it Flora?" Gretchen whispered. "Or

someone else?"

"Let's find out."

They leapt to their feet, palming the only protection they had: pepper spray. Gretchen tiptoed over, opened the door without making a sound, peeked out of the bedroom, and heard the tinkling of chimes again, the same sound that had calmed her earlier.

Her mother stayed beside her. They approached the staircase, moving silently on bare feet. The sound had started inside the room then moved into the hall. What was it?

Gretchen heard a creak below. In the dim light from the moon, she could make out the shape of someone climbing the stairs. The chimes had stopped. No one else was in the hallway with them. They waited for the person coming up the steps.

Whoever was on the stairs paused as though listening. Gretchen held her breath, taking a second to glance behind her at Caroline. The quiet, stealthy sound coming from the steps was different from the one that had alerted her mother.

Below them, the person continued up.

Gretchen had more immediate concerns than tinkling bells. Clouds passed in the sky, obscuring the moonlight and making the intruder on the steps invisible. She got ready to strike, torn with indecision.

What if the person was a friend?

But why would a friend sneak up on them?

You snuck up, she thought to herself.

Her mother touched her with a light hand. They stared at each other. Gretchen was sure they were having the same thoughts, both hesitating to harm the wrong person.

"Who's there?" Caroline said softly. "Identify yourself."

Nothing. The clouds shifted and Gretchen could see movement, still coming up at them, faster now that they'd announced their presence. A friend would have spoken up, reassured them.

They were facing an enemy.

The women nodded at each other. They released their sprays at the same time, blasting two thin directional streams. Gretchen heard a male voice, a groan. He fell to his knees three steps from the top of the landing.

Gretchen took two steps down and crouched briefly by the man, spray at the ready.

"It's Jerome," she yelled, sliding past him, almost losing her footing in her haste to get away.

"Who's Jerome?" Caroline said as they banged down the steps and ran out the door.

"The play's new light technician. He's been working with us." They stopped outside, breathing heavily. "We have to go back in."

"You're crazy," Caroline said.

"Otherwise he'll get away. We don't want that."

Caroline didn't look so sure.

Gretchen tugged on her arm. "Come on. We'll tie him up and then call the cops."

"I hate it when you're right."

"Me, too. But we don't have a choice. He'll recover and get away if we give him a chance. He has to be stopped."

"I agree. But what was that sound we heard? We didn't meet anyone when we went down the hall. What if there are two of them inside?"

"He's alone," Gretchen said. "The ghost must have alerted us."

Now she was sounding like Nina, who would have said that was the only explanation.

Caroline stared at her for a second.

"I'll deny ever saying that," Gretchen said.

"Let's get this over with," her mother said.

Jerome sat on the same step, cupping his hands over his eyes. Gretchen gave him another blast for good measure while Caroline ran to get the toolbox filled with doll repair supplies from behind the counter.

"He has a knife," Gretchen said, spotting the weapon. It was open, and close enough for him to reach it if he could see. She pushed it away with her foot, careful to avoid the blade. "A switchblade."

He moaned before reaching out to grab her ankle. She backed up. "Stay still, unless you want more of the same."

"You're making a big mistake," he said, beginning to cough.

"You aren't in any position to make threats."

Caroline came back with strips of leather, remnants left over from repairing a doll's kid-leather body. "I hate to waste it on him," she said ruefully.

Jerome tried to protest, but his eyes were clamped shut and he was overcome with uncontrollable coughing.

"I think I saw this man at the accident scene," Caroline said. "I remember the gray overalls. He was talking to a group of homeless people."

"More evidence against him."

"At least I think it's the same man." Caroline handed a piece of leather to Gretchen.

Within minutes they had Jerome trussed up like a turkey ready for the oven.

"Catching bad guys," Gretchen said,

standing back and admiring their work, "is kind of fun."

40

Gretchen stood next to the World of Dolls Museum sign. She glanced curiously at the old house's windows while her mother called to report the captured stalker.

Was he a murderer? Had he killed Allison Thomasia?

Gretchen shuddered at the thought. He had inserted himself into their group. He could have struck at any moment. Any of them might have been his next victim.

Jerome, if that was even his real name, wasn't going anyplace at the moment other than jail. Houdini wouldn't be able to get out of the knots they'd tied. Their repair expertise was paying off in more ways than one.

She wondered how long the effects of the pepper spray would last. Thirty minutes to an hour at least. Gretchen was amazed at how well it had worked, dropping him almost instantly.

Early Sunday morning and they had vindicated Allison's husband, Andy. He could come out of hiding. Gretchen was sure he'd be thrilled about that. Living with the homeless for a few days must have been quite the experience, and not one he'd be likely to want to repeat.

The early morning traffic was light since most of the downtown establishments wouldn't open until later. Gretchen glanced at her watch. Five a.m. She wished she could greet the dawn properly. If she was at the top of Camelback Mountain, she would be able to see the reddish orange glow of the sun rising from the east. In front of the museum, surrounded by buildings, the earth remained dark, except for the artificial illumination of the city's streetlights.

"The police are on their way," Caroline said, slipping her phone in a pocket, where it promptly rang again. "I shouldn't answer it," she said, digging it out and reading the information on the screen. "It's low on power."

"Who's calling?" Gretchen asked.

"I don't recognize the number."

"Better answer it."

Caroline looked tired as she clicked the Talk button. "It's Julie," she said to Gretchen after listening for a moment. "She's been doing research of her own and says that she has important information."

After another few minutes, Caroline said, "Can't you tell me on the phone?" Gretchen could hear the frustration in her voice. "We're at the museum and a little busy at the moment. We caught someone breaking in . . . We have the kill . . . All right, yes, fine."

Caroline disconnected. "Julie sounds excited and wants to meet right now. I tried to explain that we have the man who killed Allison, but she cut me off."

"She wants to meet at five in the morning? She must have worked all night. She won't come here?"

"No. She refuses to come to the Swilling house, especially with police on the way. I don't blame her."

"I'd like to run away myself," Gretchen said. "This isn't going to be pleasant."

"She says she thinks she knows who killed Allison Thomasia. She found concrete evidence against someone and wants to compare it to what we've learned. If we decide that it's important and if we agree with her, then she will come forward." Caroline looked both ways down the street. "The police should arrive momentarily. We have to stay until our statements have been recorded. She wants to meet at the banquet hall. She's on her way there and says she'll wait as long as it takes."

Gretchen heard sirens in the distance. She wasn't ready to face Matt. "I'll meet Julie. You take care of Jerome or Richard or whatever his name is, and I'll be back as soon as I can."

"You're just ducking out so you don't have to explain to your boyfriend why you tied up another man in the middle of the night." Even exhausted, her mother had enough energy to lighten the situation.

"He'd understand." *Sure, yeah, right.*

"I'm sure he would."

"Sarcasm will get you nowhere. Besides, with any luck, Matt's off duty tonight."

"You're overly optimistic. Want to bet that he shows up?"

"No bet."

"Call me when you find out what's going on with Julie."

"I don't have a phone. You made me leave it in the car."

"Take mine. I don't need it. And be careful."

"There isn't anything to be afraid of anymore," Gretchen said. "We have the killer. Hopefully Julie will have more evidence to use against him. It's over."

"Be careful anyway."

Gretchen took the cell phone and hurried down the street.

41

Terry lies in bed, staring at the ceiling. It's his day off. He should sleep the morning away and spend the rest of the afternoon reading the Sunday paper and watching old movies, but he does his best problem solving through the night. This one has been no exception. He's wide awake when his cell phone rings.

"We have a break in the case," Matt Albright says from the other end. "Evidence recovered by the ME, found at the trauma site around Allison Thomasia's head wound. Minute traces of anthropomorphized rock." His friend is speaking in choppy sentences. He's excited.

"What's that?" Terry asks. Matt is relaying the medical examiner's fancy words. She'll never learn to bring her information down to human level.

"It's residue from a rock indigenous to Israel. Now I have a pretty good idea what killed Allison Thomasia. It was the same weapon that probably killed Flora Berringer, too. A geologist's hammer."

A geologist's hammer. Or a rock pick, to be exact. When Terry was a kid, he had a brief fascination with rocks. He knows about this particular tool. The square hitting end is used to break open rock samples, to look for fossils inside. The other end of the tool, used on hard rock, is shaped like a pick for maximum striking pressure.

Matt keeps talking. "A heavy hammer like that could crush a skull without much force behind it. In the case of our killer? Lots of force was exerted, much more than required."

"Signifying uncontrolled rage," Terry says.

"Who knows what goes on inside the mind of a killer?"

Matt is like an efficient machine, narrowing down the playing field. They are eliminating suspects as quickly as possible, moving others to the top of the list.

"It should be easy from here on in," Terry says, knowing it won't be.

"Right. All we have to do is find a geologist with a motive, the rock pick that was used to kill two women, and a few missing men."

"Easy," Terry says.
"Right," Matt agrees.

42

The world is like a big picture window. You can watch people and events from the inside and remain totally invisible to those on the outside. It's like being on the observation side of a one-way mirror: hearing, seeing, waiting.

The time for waiting is over. He almost didn't recognize her. She'd changed her appearance. The hair, the clothes, the added pounds. Something in the way she walked gave her away.

Now he knows for sure, what he suspected all along.

The evil witch isn't dead. He'll never be rid of her.

She won't let up until she destroys him. Playing games, twisting the truth so he'll get the blame. He hates her with an intensity that leaves him shaking. Wicked, insane.

Memories explode randomly like they

always do when something sets him off.
Then comes the rage.

43

Why do many doll show promoters include teddy bear artists in their events? Because the two hobbies complement each other so well. Doll collectors love teddy bears. According to legend, the teddy bear got its name when President Theodore Roosevelt refused to shoot a wounded black bear. A political cartoon depicting the event inspired a store owner named Morris Michtom to create stuffed bears and display them in his shop's window as "Teddy's bears." They were an instant success, even with the fashionable ladies, who began to carry their teddies everywhere they went.

A group of teddy bears is known as "a hug." How appropriate for these cuddly adult collectibles that never go out of style!

— From *World of Dolls* by Caroline Birch

Gretchen let herself into the banquet hall,

flipped on a light in the break room, sat down in the overstuffed chair on the stage, and dozed off. She awoke to the sound of her mother's cell phone ringing and fumbled to answer it, struggling to shake off the inertia that had come with exhaustion.

"Daisy," she said when she recognized the homeless woman's voice. "Why are you calling now? It's" — she checked her watch. Nine a.m. — "early for you." Not as early as Gretchen had thought, though.

Had she really been asleep for several hours? Where was Julie? After all the drama, the woman hadn't shown up. Gretchen needed to get back to the museum. Yet she was so tired.

"Word on the street," Daisy said sounding upset, a rarity from the Red Hat Lady, "is that Jerome has been arrested."

"Yes." Gretchen's mind was still fuzzy, but clearing quickly. "How do you know him?" *Or about him?*

"He's one of us."

"Sorry to hear that he's a friend of yours," Gretchen said. "He's in deep trouble."

"He didn't do anything wrong."

"He broke into the museum and attacked us with a switchblade. And he may have killed two women already."

"No! He didn't kill anybody. He was

watching over you."

"Oh, come on."

To what extent would the homeless go to protect one another? As far as they had to?

"It's true. I sent him when I heard that you needed someone to work the stage lights. It was a perfect excuse to get someone inside to take care of you."

Gretchen stood up, began pacing the stage. "Why would I need protection?"

"Nina told me some of it, about your future. You have to get some street smarts, Gretchen."

"Apparently."

"You are going to get yourself killed if you aren't more careful. You blew it with Jerome. That was a bad call. Now the cops are going to stop looking and concentrate on making him confess." The homeless woman, usually unflappable, sounded distressed.

Why should Gretchen assume that the man creeping up the stairs with a switchblade was on her side? It couldn't possibly be true.

No. She didn't buy into the bodyguard idea. Maybe gullible Daisy believed in Jerome, but Gretchen didn't. He'd scared her from the very beginning with his sneaky ways and cold eyes.

"The cops have your mother," Daisy said.

"She's the main witness."

"They took her in."

"How do you know that?"

"My friends keep me informed. I'll get back to you when I know more. In the meantime, be careful."

Daisy disconnected, leaving Gretchen confused about many things. Daisy might sound more lucid these days, but she was clearly still paranoid and delusional.

Then she remembered Andy. She had forgotten to warn Daisy to stay away from him, to stop assisting him. Not that it mattered any longer.

The police must have needed Caroline's statement at the police station. She'd be working her way through bureaucratic red tape, trying to explain the entire story front to back. But why hadn't Caroline called Gretchen to let her know?

Maybe her mother hadn't wanted to put her through hours of tedium at the police station. Or Matt had arrived on the scene and had lost his sense of humor. Or she wanted to give Gretchen enough time to interview Julie without a battalion of law enforcement officers arriving and scaring the cop-phobic woman away.

But Julie hadn't held up her end. Where was she? Why hadn't she called?

Oh jeez.

A quick glance at the phone showed that the phone was now dead.

Gretchen was stranded at the banquet hall without a phone or transportation.

What if, a big if, Daisy was correct about Jerome? Impossible. He had come inside the museum with a knife, and he would have killed them if he'd been given the chance.

No, they couldn't have been wrong about Jerome.

She had time right now to think about the killings, to go over everything that had transpired. She selected one of Bonnie's teddy bears from the stage display. It had button-shaped eyes, plush faux fur, and a white crocheted collar with a pink bow. Gretchen made herself comfortable in the stage chair with the teddy bear in her lap and stared at the large Barbie doll.

Good thing she had locked the front door.

At least she'd done something right.

Eventually they would come looking for her. She'd stay right where she was until that happened.

44

Andy Thomasia is attempting to learn the ways of the street people, trying to blend in, to be cautious of blind alleys — and suspicious of everyone he meets. He has turned his hours of wakefulness around, sleeping through the day in one of Nacho's safe places, roaming the streets at night. He only has to do this for two days, he repeatedly tells himself.

Time's almost up.

After Gretchen left him sitting in her car in the parking lot, running away as though she had something to hide, he'd searched the car. He took her cell phone, turning it off to save on power. He scooped up quarters from the ashtray and put them in his pocket to use for bus tickets. He couldn't follow the women once they drove away in the cab, but he would use the Phoenix transportation system to search some of the places they may have gone.

He wants information from them, whatever they might have. Why would Gretchen run unless someone has turned them against him, convinced the Birches that he is guilty? Were they judging him on old evidence or on new?

He takes a bus toward the coffee shop where he first met Caroline, thinking about the woman from his past. The only thing different about Caroline since he saw her years ago is the color of her hair. And the distrustful daughter. The bus continues past the museum, where he observes a police officer getting into a squad car. What's going on there?

A few blocks later, Andy steps down from the bus. He strolls along the crosswalk toward the banquet hall. Good thing Caroline had mentioned it or he wouldn't have known where to look next.

The museum is off-limits if the cops are hanging around, that's obvious. He wonders what might have occurred there, but he doesn't dwell on it for long.

Andy leans against the entrance and peers inside through a door pane. A tiny bit of light shines down the hall, which could be anybody or nobody. But Caroline and Gretchen might be inside.

If they aren't, he'll pass the morning off

the street, waiting for them. Sunday, Gretchen had said. She would turn him in on
Sunday. He'll stay inside and call Caroline's
cell from the one he took from Gretchen's
car. When the time is right.

If they are inside, he'll deal with them.

Locks. Andy shakes his head. Not good
for squat. A lock is guaranteed to give you a
false sense of security. All he needs for this
one is a paper clip and a screwdriver, but
he has the whole lock-picking shebang. He
might as well use them, get in the fastest
way. He removes a tool from his pocket and
does a visual sweep up and down the sidewalk and street. No one notices the bum by
the door.

Andy rakes the lock by inserting a pick
into the keyhole. Then he pulls it out
quickly, hearing the click of the pins. Next
he turns the plug with a tension wrench and
grins with satisfaction.

That's all it takes. He's inside.

45

Gretchen finished off another cup of coffee and started a fresh pot. Nothing like caffeine to get her mind working in full throttle. She'd gone over the past week's events, recalling as many little nuances as possible, noting anything and everything unusual, which turned out to be most of it. Her aunt Gertie had been wise with her advice. Any time her instincts had set off an alarm in her head, any time she thought connections weren't logical, she made another mental note.

She wanted to prove without a doubt that Jerome was a killer. Could she work through events and verify it by eliminating some of the other suspects?

But the task got too large. Her head couldn't hold it all, especially after the long sleepless night. She went to pen and paper, using her newly acquired family tree–building skills to form branches for murder suspects.

She began one limb of the tree by writing in names of the attorney and the newest trust beneficiary: Dean McNalty and Trudy Fernwich. But Gretchen had few observations to work with. A woman she'd never met who wanted to remain anonymous had hired an attorney to keep her identity secret and to make the museum happen.

If Dean McNalty wanted to eliminate the Swilling trust beneficiaries, he would have killed Trudy Fernwich, not Allison Thomasia.

Trudy Fernwich might have killed Allison, but Caroline had also been attacked. Would the Fernwich woman have offered the doll club the opportunity to convert the house only to turn around and try to kill them? Not likely.

She crossed off McNalty and Fernwich.

Jerome had a switchblade and a bad attitude. He was her first pick. But Daisy didn't think he'd done anything wrong, and Daisy wasn't easily fooled. She also had that unexplained networking thing going on. Could their drums beat out the name of the real killer if the homeless community needed to know? Gretchen wouldn't be surprised.

Then she remembered her mother's comment about Jerome. She had seen him at the accident, speaking with the homeless. His presence established evidence against him, suggesting that he was following Caroline. It could also be the basis for his innocence, if Daisy was correct about his role as protector.

Next, Gretchen wrote down the names of the doll club members, but she quickly eliminated them. After all, they were her friends. They were working hard to make the fundraiser a success.

Her pen wavered above Julie's name. Julie Wicker was the peacemaker of the group, running interference between the director and the cast, always having a kind word to say. So why hadn't Julie met her as she said she would? What did she know? Gretchen prayed that Julie hadn't been murdered for what she knew. She didn't want the reason to take Julie's name off of the list to be because she'd been killed.

What about Andy? He didn't have an alibi, and he'd left identification at the cemetery like a calling card. And he and his wife were estranged when she died.

Andy and Jerome were tied for first place.

But Andy hadn't attacked her with a weapon as Jerome had. Thinking back on the encounter, Jerome hadn't exactly attacked them. He hadn't even put up much resistance. Gretchen's adrenaline had been pumping hard at the time. Now she wondered if her mother and she had initiated the assault.

The more she thought, the more confused she became.

While she was at it, she might as well add the ghost to the murder tree she was creating. What if the apparition held a grudge against the family and would haunt them forever, killing descendants in bloody revenge? Gretchen didn't write that down. It was too far out in Ninaland for her.

Gretchen left the coffee pot to work its magic brew and returned to the comfort of the stage chair.

That's when she heard a soft click coming from down the hall.

46

Gretchen ducked into the break room and pressed her body up behind the door, one eye staring out from the crack. Heavy footsteps slowly approached.

A cold blast of intuition had propelled Gretchen out of the chair and off the stage, telling her to seek shelter. *Hurry.* She reacted to the perceived threat and ran, now feeling slightly foolish for hiding behind a door.

She'd lost all perspective. She was running scared instead of standing and fighting. Yet she wasn't about to come out without knowing who was inside the room.

Through the crack in the door, she watched and waited. Footsteps paused. She flattened herself further. Whoever was inside the building was as wary as she.

The footsteps continued forward until he came into view.

Andy Thomasia!

The man had a way of working with locks

that frightened her. What was wrong with him that he couldn't respect a locked door? He was carrying a weapon of some sort, holding it in his right hand as though he expected to use it soon.

The silence was so absolute, Gretchen was sure he'd hear her if she swallowed or blinked. She froze, motionless like the six-foot Barbie on the stage that had caught his attention. She had a moment to think of her next move while he stepped up on the stage and walked around the enormous doll.

She didn't have anything to protect herself with. Where was her pepper spray? Gretchen couldn't remember what she'd done with it after spraying Jerome.

Daisy had been right about Jerome. Now that she was locked in a deserted building with the murdered woman's husband, she believed Daisy.

Too late.

Think! How am I going to escape?

Andy's gaze found the teddy bear lying on the floor in front of the chair that Gretchen had so hastily abandoned. He swung his head toward the break room, alert again, hunting for sound or motion. He cocked his head, his eyes sweeping along the floor from the stage to the door where Gretchen hid.

She pressed against the wall.

318

His eyes followed the crack in the door from the bottom up. He looked sinister, gaunt and menacing.

Their eyes locked.

"Don't come down from the stage," Gretchen said. "Or I'll shoot."

"You're the exact image of your mother. Feisty, passionate." Andy moved fluidly down the stage steps. "Impulsive."

"I mean it. Stop."

"You don't have a gun."

"I do."

"Show me."

"I don't take orders from you."

Oh jeez.

"Where's Caroline?" he asked.

"She'll be here any minute with the police."

Where are you, Mom?

Andy looked a little worn around the edges. Under different circumstances, Gretchen would have felt sorry for him. That is, if he hadn't been so adept at breaking and entering. And if his driver's license hadn't been left at the scene of the murder. "What happened at the museum?" he asked.

"Why?"

"I saw a cop leaving."

"I don't know what happened," Gretchen lied.

My mother and I decided to beat up the wrong guy.

"Come out from behind the door," Andy said. "We need to talk."

"I wouldn't have helped you in the first place if I knew then what I know now."

"Somebody is setting me up. You have to believe me."

"Go away. Tell that to the police."

"Come out and talk to me."

"Yeah, right, like I'll trot right over and let you stab me."

Andy scowled. Then he glanced at the thing in his hand. "Oh, this? It's my lock pick." He put it in his pocket and held up his hands as though that would reassure her.

Gretchen, still flattened against the wall behind the door, looked back into the break room, frantic to find a weapon and protect herself. Where was the stage pistol? That would get her out of here. He wouldn't know that it was a fake.

The gun wasn't in sight.

"I tell you what," Andy said, taking one slow step at a time toward her, "I'll come in there and we'll have a cup of that wonderful-smelling coffee and share information."

"Stay out. I'm warning you."

"But I'm turning myself in, right? I'm giving myself up to you."

He came closer, reached the threshold. When he walked through the doorway, Gretchen used all her might to slam the door against him. She locked both palms against the back of the door and shoved as hard as she could, throwing all her body weight behind it.

She felt resistance, but she'd expected that. If his reflexes were slower than hers, the door might hit him in the head. That didn't happen. Instead, the door was coming back at her.

They were locked in a war against each other. He, on the outside, determined to get in. She, on the inside, doing everything she could to keep him out.

Gretchen was a strong woman. She'd been jealous of all the Phoenix twig women when she had first arrived in Arizona, but now, she thanked her body. Heavier would have been even better. Three hundred pounds would have been perfect.

She was no match for Andy. He had the advantage of additional weight and more arm strength.

He was going to kill her after he won this last arm-wrestling bout.

She felt the door inching back at her, heard both of them breathing hard, felt her feet sliding back, and looked around one last time for a weapon.

Then she was flung away and the door banged against the wall, wide open.

"I don't have time for this," Andy snarled, coming at her. "You're going to tell me what you know, if I have to force it out of you."

Gretchen grabbed the first thing she saw, the first thing she could get in her grasp, and whipped it at him. The coffeepot crashed into Andy and a wave of hot coffee shot from the rim.

He slapped his hands against his face, trying to wipe away the hot brew.

"Strike one," she screamed, feeling warriorlike in spite of her terror. The coffeepot shattered on the floor, but she was already moving, picking up a heavy mug and throwing it at him, striking his forehead. She wasn't going down without a fight. She'd make sure to scratch him. They would find traces of his DNA under her fingernails. She'd figure out how to leave a message before she died.

She backed toward a small, cluttered table in the corner. Stage props were piled on it, and she almost collapsed in joy when she saw the butt of the stage gun poking out of the mess.

Gretchen grabbed the gun and trained it on Andy. "Turn around slowly," she said.

322

"Do it!"

That stopped him. Without another word, he did as she demanded, turning his back to her. He looked overly confident for a man in his position. His hands were in his pockets. The pick!

Without further thought, she clunked him on the head with the gun. He wobbled. She drew back and struck again, harder this time. He crashed to the floor.

Standing over his prone body, Gretchen hoped she hadn't hit him too hard. What if she'd killed him?

Andy didn't move.

Was he breathing?

Gretchen wasn't about to get close enough to find out or to be grabbed.

She'd call the cops and an ambulance.

Should she run out into the street and flag someone down?

She'd get Mr. B. He'd help her.

Gretchen pounded up the stairs and rapped hard on Mr. B.'s apartment door, watching her back all the way, feeling afraid, feeling the adrenaline.

47

Mr. B. didn't answer her desperate knocks. She turned the doorknob.

Unlocked.

What a break.

If he wasn't at home, she could still go inside and use his phone. He'd never know, and if he did, he'd understand that she'd had no choice. Gretchen opened the door cautiously, not wanting to startle Mr. B. if he was home. "It's Gretchen," she called, trying to project her voice out, but not loud enough to give her location away to Andy. "I need to use your phone."

Gretchen quickly shut the door behind her and locked it, loving the sound of the bolt action. Then she remembered Andy's lock-picking tool. He still had it.

Move quickly, she told herself. Although he hadn't looked like he was in any shape to pursue her.

She looked around at the typical single

older male décor, stark in contrast to what he'd accomplished with the lower banquet hall. The smell of pipe tobacco hung in the air, thick and soothing.

Gretchen moved through the apartment, still calling out softly while glancing around for a landline. A younger man might not have one in these modern days of high-tech advancement and wireless connections, but Gretchen had noticed Mr. B.'s old-fashioned mannerisms and she'd never seen him using a cell phone.

He'd have a landline phone in his house.

The small kitchen and living area didn't produce one.

The door to the only other room in the apartment was closed. She tapped. Nothing from inside.

Slowly she turned the handle.

What would he think if he came home and found her inside, searching through his house? How embarrassing would that be?

Gretchen poked her head inside. His bedroom. Drawn blinds on the windows kept the room cast in darkness, but she could tell that it wasn't occupied at the moment. She flipped a switch on the wall next to the door and an overhead light came on.

There had better be a phone in here or she'd have to go back down those steps and risk another encounter with Andy. That is, if she hadn't killed him.

For good measure, she also locked the bedroom door behind her. That would slow down the professional lock picker.

The nightstand didn't offer up a phone. Neither did the top of the dresser.

The man didn't have a phone? What was the world coming to?

In the future, she'd be telling her children old-fashioned stories of street-side pay phones and phones with cords. If she lived to have kids.

Gretchen's eyes lit on a glass curio cabinet in the corner that she hadn't noticed at first. She walked over, peered in — and sucked in her breath in surprise.

The cabinet contained rocks, a fairly sizeable collection. Each specimen had an identification tag attached to it.

Gretchen opened the curio and picked up a rock. Read the tag.

Exchanged it for another. Read another tag.

And another.

The rocks had long complex names that she couldn't pronounce, let alone decipher. Granodiorite, gabbro, anaorthosite gneiss.

And every one of them had a place of origin neatly printed underneath the name.

Cairo.

Jericho.

Zimbabwe.

The same exotic places she'd daydreamed about. The travel stickers had come from these faraway cities. They had been placed lovingly on a doll's travel trunk by a young girl named Flora.

Gretchen had found John Swilling's rock collection.

48

Caroline sits in an interrogation room with Matt Albright. Good thing Gretchen took off down the street before the detective found out about their escapade at the museum. He's working his jaw like he's trying to restrain an angry outburst. It crosses her mind to push him a little. What happens when her daughter's boyfriend gets really angry? She'd like to see him at his worst.

If he's not the right guy for Gretchen, she wants to know now.

"Let me get this straight," he says. "You spent the night at the museum after I specifically told you that it was off-limits?"

"You never told me any such thing."

"I warned your daughter. The two of you violated police orders. That building is under investigation. It's a crime scene. I can't believe it." He studies the ceiling like he might find the answer written up there.

Caroline feels a tinge of compassion for him. He's in a tough place, sitting on the fence between his professional ethics and his personal relationship with her daughter. Would he be exhibiting this kind of frustration with two women he didn't know? She doesn't think so. He feels helpless and is afraid for them. His emotions surface as anger. She studied psychology in college and is putting it to good use.

She won't let him get to her.

His elbows are on the table. He rubs both hands through his hair. "Where is she?" he asks.

"I said I'll tell you but not yet." *Calm down first.*

"The guy you hog-tied insists he was protecting you."

"Hardly likely. He broke in. He had a knife."

"You think he's a killer."

"Yes."

"Both Flora Berringer and Allison Thomasia were murdered with a geologist's hammer, not a switchblade. The killer didn't use a knife on his victims. The guy you assaulted is in trouble for breaking and entering and carrying, but not for murdering a woman in a cemetery. Not for stashing bones in an armoire."

Could Matt be right? Caroline isn't sure. But Jerome, not exactly a harmless guy, is off the street. "I wouldn't discount him if I were you," she says.

"Where is she?"

"At the banquet hall. She has my cell phone."

She gives him the number and he dials with his thumb. "No answer."

"The phone was running low on power."

They are out in a front entry room of the police station when another cop pulls Matt aside. Whispers. She hears only one word. *Berringer.*

"I'll have someone take you home," Matt says to her. "I'll let you know if we need anything else from you."

He has dismissed her, distracted.

The detective stops at a window and speaks clearly, so Caroline doesn't miss a word. "Locate a car in central Phoenix," he says to the dispatcher. "Have the squad pick up Gretchen Birch and bring her here." He gives the location of the banquet hall before disappearing down the hall.

49

Gretchen was rigid with shock. She stared at the rock collection. It had to be John Swilling's collection. What was it doing in Mr. B.'s apartment? Was her landlord actually Richard Berringer? No wonder the man had been so eager to donate space for their luncheon. The club members had been thrilled. They wouldn't have considered turning down his offer. How devious!

She glanced out the window to the street below. A car pulled up on the side of the building and Julie Wicker got out of the driver's side.

A little late for their meeting, but Gretchen would forgive the woman for not showing up earlier. She needed her help and was relieved to see her alive and well.

She raised the blind. The window rolled open easily. Gretchen called out to her. "Am I glad to see you!"

Julie looked up, startled. "What are you

doing up there?"

"It's a long story. I have to get out of here immediately. Do you have a phone?"

"Of course."

"I'll be right down."

"Are you alone?"

"No, I mean, yes, but if I don't come out in the next two minutes, call the police. Wait. Call them anyway."

Julie said something else, but Gretchen couldn't hear because she was already at the bedroom door, then at the apartment door, then creeping quickly down the steps straining her ears for any sound of movement below.

She thought she heard something. Before letting herself out, she peeked cautiously into the break room. Andy sat on the floor, moaning and holding his head.

What if he had a concussion? "An ambulance will be on the way soon," she said. He nodded weakly.

She had to get medical attention for him.

The warm sunny day shocked Gretchen after so much time spent indoors in low lighting. She blinked like a mole.

"What in the world is going on?" Julie asked.

"I need to use your phone. I might have made a terrible mistake. A man inside might die because of me."

"Mr. B.? What did you do to Mr. B.?"

Gretchen shook her head in frustration. "Not Mr. B., Andy Thomasia. I thought he killed his wife. I hit him pretty hard with the stage gun. We have to call an ambulance."

"What can I do?" Julie said.

"Stay with me. I don't know what's going on anymore. But I'm pretty sure that Mr. B., the guy who owns this building, is Richard Berringer."

"Impossible," Julie said.

"He has his grandfather's rock collection upstairs."

"No!"

"Give me the phone."

"I'll take care of it." Julie keyed in the emergency number and spoke into the phone, giving their location and requesting an ambulance to assist with an injured man inside the building. "Now we can relax," she said after hanging up.

"Perfect. Let's go in and wait with Andy."

"The ambulance attendants will take good care of him. There isn't anything we can do. And if the man who lives upstairs really is Richard, we could be in significant danger. We need to get away."

Julie looked frightened. *She should be,*

Gretchen thought. *We both should be.*

Gretchen chewed the inside of her lip and considered the dilemma. There wasn't anything she could do about Andy's condition. And she wasn't absolutely sure that he hadn't killed his wife. And what about Mr. B.? Owning a rock collection wasn't enough evidence to assume that Mr. B. was a killer. Was it?

She had made too many assumptions as it was.

"Okay," Gretchen said, scanning the street for signs of Mr. B. "Let's get in your car. We'll lock ourselves in."

Was that enough protection? The killer had rammed her mother's car in an attempt to murder her. Would he do the same to them if he found them here?

Looking up and down the street again, she didn't see Mr. B., but he could turn a corner at any moment. Had any of the club members asked what his full name was? Yes, she remembered that April had. He'd said it was a long Slavic name, that everyone called him Mr. B.

"Where's Caroline?" Julie asked.

"Another long story. I'll tell you later. Why don't we move the car?"

Julie nodded, checking out passing pedestrians. "I agree. We can wait down the street for the ambulance to arrive. Or drive around the block. Or something. But we shouldn't stand in the open like sitting ducks."

The temporary security of Julie's car gave Gretchen a moment to reflect on her own impulsive personality, and how much trouble she had caused. First Jerome, then Andy. She was leaving a trail of carnage behind her.

Matt had been right all along. She shouldn't have involved herself in police business. But to be fair, Gretchen didn't invite threats. They appeared out of nowhere. She'd been perfectly content working on the play, minding her own business.

Well, that wasn't exactly true. The drama of past and present mysterious murders had lured her away. She'd wanted to be enticed into something else. Anything other than directing that play.

So she'd seen a killer in every man she encountered. She'd disarmed one and tied him up. She'd pistol-whipped another.

Was she the crazy one?

Julie was on the phone talking to the police, explaining that their lives were at risk, that a man might be stalking them and that they needed protection. She sounded more worried and frightened as she spoke.

"Yes, yes, we will. No, that's not possible."

She glanced at Gretchen and covered the phone with her hand. "I'm not going to the police station, which is what they are suggesting."

"What's wrong with that?" Gretchen asked, recalling that Julie had refused to go to the museum the night before because of the police. "We'll be safest there."

"No. I have an issue with that. I'll drop you off, though."

"Let's stay together."

"Should we wait here?" Julie asked. "The officer thinks it will be fifteen or twenty minutes."

"How about at the museum?" Even if Mr. B. was Richard, the club had changed the locks to the museum and only Gretchen and her mother had keys. "He can't get into the museum."

"Great idea." Julie gave the address to the police officer and hung up. "A police car is on the way. They said to stay inside."

It would be over before she knew it. In fifteen minutes the police would arrive, if they weren't still there. Hadn't Andy said he'd seen a cop at the museum? All her potential suspects were being rounded up. She may have been mistaken in some cases and injured the wrong people, but one of them was guilty. Andy Thomasia, Jerome, or

Mr. B. One of them was a killer. It was really over this time.

50

"She has multiple personalities," Richard Berringer says while the technician sits at a computer. The detective remains standing, appears detached. People probably lie to him all the time. Best to focus on the truth and keep an honest face.

"Her head is in a good place when she remembers to take her medication," he says, studying the black Velcro wrapped around his fingers. "But that's hit-or-miss. When we were kids, before the meds, Rachel would do cruel things and then blame me. Everybody believed her, including my parents. She'd do horrible things to animals and kids too young to talk, then she'd blame me. She nearly suffocated herself and accused me of attempting to kill her. That was the end for me."

Richard hasn't moved since he sat down in the chair, not a muscle, but the detective — what's his name . . . Albright? — paces.

The cop's voice and facial features don't display any emotion, no inflections whatsoever. He sounds like the computer program that they are running to record his blood pressure and pulse, to verify the truth.

How can his blood pressure not be through the roof? But they told him he passed the pretest with flying colors. And they have control questions. It's all been explained to him. He's more than willing to go along, whatever it takes to make them believe him.

He's careful to conceal his anger, to not let it control him. That's how she won before, driving him to the point of explosive rage.

"Anything to make me look bad," he continues, trying not to reflect too much on his sister and the memories that are surfacing like monsters from the depths of a lagoon. "When I was a teenager, my parents had me committed to an insane asylum. As bad as it was, it was better than living in the same house with her. Two years later, I was out, but I didn't go home. I kept in touch with my parents, though. By then they knew the truth about Rachel, but they didn't send her away. She got shock treatments instead. At least I escaped that."

Richard's voice is becoming emotional.

He has pent-up anger, but he can't let them see the rage. The detective leans against the back of a chair, hunches his shoulders forward to stretch his neck muscles. "Go on," he says.

"When our mother disappeared, I knew Rachel must have killed her. I came back to Phoenix and told the police my suspicions, but I was the one who had been institutionalized, not Rachel. Nothing came of it.

"Some unexplainable force wouldn't let me leave this city. I hated the house and all its memories, but I couldn't run away from my past. I bought the building I own now, paid it off as quick as I could. Rachel owned the family home, although she didn't live in it. We kept our distance from each other."

"She didn't bother you?"

"Not really. She had become good at hiding the crazy side. She said she had a therapist and the right medications. I didn't see her much. Then recently I heard that she had died."

The detective glances at the technician then back to Richard. "Could you get to the point, please? I understand that your sister did you a huge injustice, but if she's dead —"

Richard shakes his head. *They have to believe me! Otherwise she will have won again.* "That's what I'm trying to tell you," he says. "She had different personalities. She could be anybody she wanted to be. She killed that woman in the cemetery and faked her own death. She's still in Phoenix, but she isn't Rachel Berringer anymore."

Another glance between the two men. Richard wants to rip off the polygraph equipment and run away. They aren't believing his story. He never should have come here.

"Explain," Albright says.

"Rachel isn't really dead. I'm telling you the truth. She's simply taken on a different personality."

"And what would that personality be?"

Richard leans in closer.

"She's become someone else, one of our relatives," he says. "And she will kill again, if we don't stop her."

"Give me a name to go on."

"Julie Wicker," Richard says.

Gretchen unlocked the museum door, disappointed that the police weren't there to greet them. "I'm going to wait outside," she said, watching Julie pull a large tote out of the backseat and walk up the sidewalk toward her. The woman carried a ton of stuff. Not that Gretchen should talk. She usually had Nimrod and all his supplies with her.

She felt a pang of loneliness, missing her lovable creatures. Wobbles and Nimrod. What a pair.

"The police told us to wait inside," Julie said.

"I need fresh air. Don't worry about me. I'll stay close by the door."

"Call me when the police arrive," Julie said. "I've been so busy with the play, I haven't had time to go through the museum."

"Sure. Take your time, but watch out for

the ghost." Gretchen tried to make light.

"Ghost?" Julie stopped. "I forgot that the house is supposed to be haunted."

Gretchen grinned. "That's what Nina thinks. Remember? She insists that Flora's spirit is trapped between two worlds, that she has unfinished business on earth and that her spirit needs to be reconnected somehow."

Reconnected to her head, Gretchen thought, *but that's morbid and Julie seems nervous as it is.*

Gretchen didn't tell Julie that she believed right along with Nina that the house was haunted. Hadn't strange noises alerted them to the contents of the armoire? And later hadn't chimes warned of Jerome's presence? If not for the intervention of the ghost, they may have been killed.

She wasn't ready, though, to announce it to the world.

"Maybe I won't go inside after all."

"No, really, it's nothing to be afraid of," Gretchen said. "If the house has a ghost, I'm sure it's a benevolent ghost. I'll come inside, turn on lights for you, and we'll prove that the building is safe."

"Okay. Let's do it."

Julie stepped over the threshold.

So did Gretchen.

52

"Last year," Richard says after Detective Albright refills their coffee cups, "she gave me my father's rock collection." The technician is done. Richard's fingers are free. "I was so grateful. Finally, a piece of family history, a small treasure, for myself. But then I couldn't help thinking that she had a motive for that generosity."

The detective seems to perk up at the reference to rocks and asks Richard about his father's work, which Richard expands on. "He traveled most of the time, one geological dig after another."

"And the equipment? What happened to his tools?"

"I don't know. Maybe she has them, or they still could be in the house. Nothing was ever thrown out." That's the truth. All those dolls and the same furnishings. The secrets are still there, too.

"I'd like permission to search your home,"

the detective says. "Do you have a problem with that?"

"No," Richard says. "All I had to hide was my institutional history and my insane sister, and even that's out in the open now."

Richard is left alone while the search is arranged. The lock on the interrogation room clicks into place, trapping him. He wonders how long Rachel has been a member of the doll club, masquerading as Julie Wicker. Just like Rachel to gravitate to a bunch of doll enthusiasts.

He has nothing left to hide from the police, his soul has been stripped bare, but he's worried anyway. What if they find something inside his house that they can use against him?

Stranger things have happened.

Paranoid tendencies, that's what the doc said. Richard's never been able to trust anybody. How can he start now?

"Richard," Albright says from the doorway, "I'd like you to come along with us."

"Of course." *Be agreeable.*

Richard sits in the backseat of a squad car. A uniformed police officer is driving. Albright gets into the passenger seat. Richard thinks of another story to tell on the way over to search his house. One he's been saving for last. This will seal the deal. They have to believe him now.

"One of those doll women came to the hall early this morning," he says. "I saw her go in from my window. Then, a little while later, Rachel showed up."

"She did? No kidding."

"I thought I'd spotted her on the street outside the hall the day before, walking with some of the others, but I wasn't certain. She'd changed her appearance. It was the eyes that gave her away. She has my mother's eyes, the shape, the color, everything the same. *But Rachel's dead,* I said to myself. I didn't want to face the truth."

"That must have been a shock."

You bet it was. "I knew she was up to no good, either following the other woman or after me for something." He laughs a sad sound. "With all my talk, you must think I'm paranoid."

"Not at all." But he hears the agreement in the detective's voice. "What happened next?"

"I opened the window and told Rachel to get back in her car and get away from my building. I told her I'd call the cops. That's when I knew for certain it was her under the dyed black hair and different clothes. She said she knew I didn't have a phone, which was true. Hate the things. Salespeople

346

and political calls. Who needs it? I held up my television remote and told her I had bought one. She thought it was a phone in the dark and left real quick."

"What morning was this?"

"This morning."

"This morning?" The detective swings his head to the backseat. "Are you sure?"

"Why wouldn't I remember when it happened? I'm telling you it was today. That's why I came here. We have to stop her."

It has taken a whole lot of work to get a reaction from the detective. Finally he has one. Albright is paying attention.

"What about the woman who went inside?" he asks Richard. "Who was she?"

"Don't know. They all look the same to me."

"What did she look like? Tall? Short? Heavy? Come on."

Richard describes the early-morning visitor. "Young, thirtyish. She's the one directing the play for that bunch of doll collectors."

"Gretchen."

"You know her?"

"Speed it up," the detective says to the driver.

At last! Richard thinks. *Action!*

53

Julie placed her tote on the museum counter and looked around at the doll displays. "Caroline really does great work," she said. "With one of the largest collections in Phoenix, this will be a wonderful museum."

Gretchen turned on more lights. Her eyes shifted automatically to the staircase where she'd last seen Jerome. She didn't want to remember last night, the sheer terror as she and her mother had waited for the intruder to climb the steps.

"Let's go upstairs," Julie said.

"We better wait by the door. The police will be here soon." Gretchen had had enough of the upstairs. A skeleton found in the closet and a scuffle with an intruder were plenty for her.

"Oh come on."

"No, really."

Julie looked up the spiral staircase. "I'm not going up alone if there's a ghost around.

From what I've read, they like to roam on second stories near bedrooms."

Gretchen had heard that, too. And the ghostly sounds had occurred upstairs, so there must be some truth to it.

"Most of the finished work is in the rooms down here anyway," she pointed out to Julie. "Contemporaries are down the hall to the left, antiques to the right. But you know that."

"Yes." Julie smiled. "I helped April for a few hours, but I'd like to see them again. If you hear me scream, come and save me."

Gretchen grinned. "Take your time."

While Julie explored the house, Gretchen sat down on a stool by the counter. Shouldn't she hear ambulance sirens by now? How long had it been? It felt like hours, but had probably only been a few minutes.

Julie's cell phone was on the counter next to the tote. She picked it up and checked the time. Almost eleven. She was impatient to put this all behind her. And to get some sleep.

She checked the cell's call log to get the specific time of both calls, the one requesting an ambulance for Andy and the second call requesting police protection at the museum.

That's odd, she thought. *The calls weren't logged.*

But Gretchen had heard Julie's end of the conversations.

Had she been pretending to make the calls?

Gretchen glanced down the hall. "Aren't they wonderful?" she called out to get a sense of Julie's location.

"Yes." Julie's voice came from one of the far rooms.

"Take your time. The police certainly are."

Julie hadn't called for help. Why?

Then she realized that Julie had understood exactly what Gretchen meant when they met at the banquet hall and she told Julie that she'd found Richard and the rock collection. Hadn't Julie been in Tucson when they had canvassed the neighborhood and discovered personal information about Richard and Rachel? April and Nina had agreed to keep their findings a secret.

Then how did Julie know she should be afraid of Richard? How did she know about John Swilling's collection?

Although Julie had been researching on her own. That's why she had wanted to meet them at the banquet hall, to share information. What had kept her away? What did she know?

Gretchen heard footsteps coming back down the hall. She hastily put down the phone. Julie slung the tote over her shoulder, put the phone in her pocket, and headed for the stairs. "Let's go visit a ghost," she said. "I can't resist."

"I thought you were afraid to go up there."

"I am, but curious as well. What if the spirit is Rachel's? Wouldn't that be something? To speak with her?"

"How do you know that Rachel is dead?"

"I looked it up. That's part of what we need to talk about. But right now, let's visit the upstairs."

"I'll wait here."

Gretchen watched her make her way up the staircase. What was the woman up to? Was she going to steal something? She better not take the travel trunk. Instinct told Gretchen to be careful, that the woman knew more than she was letting on. Gretchen had to try to find out what she was hiding.

On the way upstairs, Gretchen walked quietly along the edge of the risers careful not to make any sound that would warn Julie of her approach. The woman might have wanted to find a way into the house to recover an object. But what?

Gretchen slid along the hall and peered

into the storage room where she had left the trunk on top of a display case. It was still there. Julie hadn't been after Flora's little travel trunk.

What then? Was she helping Richard? But Julie seemed so sweet, always making sure the women got along, smoothing ruffled feathers.

She should get out of here. Why hadn't she waited outside? But what good would that have done? Julie hadn't called the police. They weren't coming to rescue her.

Fear crept into Gretchen's thoughts. Julie had wanted her inside the house. Why? Was Richard here? Julie had coaxed until Gretchen had fallen right in with her. She'd followed like a lamb to slaughter.

Ghost, she thought, *why didn't you warn me like you did when Jerome broke in? Where are you?*

"Gretchen." Julie stood in the doorway. "There you are. I've been looking for you."

54

The proper tools and supplies are an important part of a doll restoration artist's trade. You never know when and where they will come in handy, so my advice is to have equipment for simple repairs readily accessible. When traveling, a small kit or toolbox fits compactly in the trunk of a car. Portable repair items should include the basics: restringing elastic, a variety of hooks, cleaning products and cloths, needles, threads, glue, and cotton swabs. Most restoration artists find themselves adding other useful items to their traveling inventory as they expand their services.

— From *World of Dolls* by Caroline Birch

Julie's eyes narrowed as she came into the room. Gretchen thought everything about the woman had become more sinister, darker and more suspicious, as if she could read Gretchen's thoughts and found them unacceptable. But Gretchen had to play along for now. "I'm going back down to wait," she said.

"There's nothing to wait for, but you suspected that already. No one is coming to rescue you."

"What do you mean?" Gretchen backed up, squeezing through the tightly stacked boxes, trying to put distance between them.

"Richard is going to kill you the same way he killed his mother."

Richard *was* inside the museum! And Julie was helping him!

"Where is he?" Gretchen asked, straining to hear the sound of another set of footsteps.

"All the clues will point to him. I even have his pipe and tobacco." Julie produced a small pouch from a pocket. Gretchen recognized it as the same kind that Mr. B. used. She'd watched him stoke his pipe, knew his preference. "That nice cherry aroma should cling in the air long enough. That'll be the end of him."

"Who are you?" Gretchen said. This wasn't the same doll collector that she'd known through the club. This woman's face was flushed with rage, almost unrecognizable as Julie's.

"I went out of my way to set up that woman's husband," Julie continued. "That bumbling fool I hired stole his license and was supposed to drop it near the body. He botched the job, but there's still hope."

"And now you intend to kill me and blame Richard?"

Blame Richard. The elderly neighborhood women had talked about how they'd learned of Richard's violent nature through stories told by Rachel. Isn't that what they'd said? Had the sister been lying to everyone about her brother?

Several things clicked into place at once. What proof did Gretchen have that verified Rachel's death? None at all. All it had taken to convince her of the woman's demise was an obituary in the local paper.

Julie came closer, weaving through the storage boxes, carrying something that Gretchen hadn't noticed at first, some kind of hammer with a sharp, pointed end. "You had no business coming into my home," Julie said. "It belongs to me. You and your mother deserve whatever you get. You had your warning, just like that woman from California had hers."

"The note on my windshield?"

"You still wouldn't stop, even when you knew what would happen if you didn't."

"How could I know?" *Humor her.* Gretchen had to try to get through to the Julie she had known.

"The first time that woman visited the attorney, I knew that Rachel had to die. The California snoop wouldn't go away, wouldn't stop asking questions about my mother. I'd been toying with the idea of permanently assuming Julie's identity. You can't imagine how tiring it was to keep up two roles. It turned out to be easy to kill off Rachel as well as my past. Just like that . . ." She snapped her fingers. "Everything erased."

Julie's eyes looked wild, like those of a rabid predator. She was a large woman with a lot of bulk. If she struck Gretchen with the hammer, that would be the end for her. But Julie seemed content to tell her story. At least for a few minutes longer. "Allison wasn't next in line to inherit the house, so she wasn't a threat in that respect. But she was trying to get inside the house. For what? She must have suspected something. Then she started talking about Rachel, wanting to get a copy of the death certificate. She wouldn't quit. When she wanted to see the graves, I offered to meet her in the old part of the cemetery and introduce her to the end of a family line."

"You struck her with that?" Gretchen pointed at the hammer. Julie had such a

356

tight grip on it, her knuckles were white.

"I didn't want to dishonor my family's resting place, but I had to act fast."

"That's why you tried to kill her at a different grave site? You didn't want to desecrate their graves? *She was crazier than Gretchen had first thought!*

"The little fool crawled in spite of her injuries."

Stay calm. Play for time. "Why did you write the words on the tombstone? Why Die, Dolly, Die?"

"My dear little relative had several phone conversations with the new me. We were very chummy. She told me that Dolly was her husband's pet name for her. The police were so inept. It should have been their first indication that the husband was involved."

"I had no idea what was going on." If only the woman would stop staring at her with madness in her eyes. "I'm sorry we caused you so much anguish. Of course, we will return the house to you immediately."

"Turn and face the wall," Julie said. "It will be over quickly. You won't feel a thing. One minute you'll be alive, the next you'll be gone, no conscious thought left. Won't that be a relief, to be out of this cruel world forever, just like Mommy?"

Gretchen needed to find a weapon of her

357

own. Her mother had left a few doll supplies on top of one of the boxes, but they
weren't a match for the heavy hammer.

She looked into Julie's eyes, refusing to
show fear. "No," she said. "I'm not going to
turn my back. That's how you killed Allison, by sneaking up behind her. You killed
your mother the same way. What a coward
you are, Rachel.

"I can understand why you killed your
mother." *Yeah, right.* "But why try to harm
my mother? Why write Die, Dolly, Die and
put it under my windshield wiper?"

"You couldn't understand how I felt when
Mommy started talking as though I was the
one with problems. I was always the good
one, not Richard. How could she want to
put me away? If only she hadn't forced me
to hurt her."

"But why my mother? Why try to kill her?"

"She didn't belong in my house. Neither
did you. I thought Julie was the next in line
to inherit the house. I never heard of anyone
named Trudy Fernwich. As it turned out,
Mommy had secrets of her own, relatives
she never told me about. That woman
shouldn't have given my house to the club
to turn into a museum. You and your mother
should have stayed away but you wouldn't.
It's your fault that I had to disturb Mommy,

why I had to try to move her to another resting place."

Gretchen didn't want to consider the extent of this mad woman's rage at learning that the home had slipped through her fingers. She didn't want to think about Flora's head, either. All this death and destruction because of one woman's uncontrolled madness.

Rachel's mother was dead because of what she knew. Allison was dead because of what Rachel thought she knew. Gretchen and her mother were next in line for termination because of a simple act of generosity from the new owner. And what about Trudy Fernwich? Would she be next?

If Gretchen didn't survive, who would warn Caroline?

Julie wasn't moving, but her eyes were wary. "I need to know where Trudy Fernwich is. Tell me, and I'll consider letting you live."

"I don't know where she is." She had to find a weapon.

"The house has to stay in the family. It belongs to me, not to her."

Without any warning, Julie lunged forward, bringing the hammer up over her shoulder. For a heavy woman she was quick. Gretchen saw the flat side of the hammer descending toward her and moved sideways, trying to dodge the blow. The weapon slammed into her left shoulder. Gretchen went down, feeling pain and hearing the bone crack.

Her mother's repair supplies had fallen with her. A can of enamel spray paint rolled toward her. What would a shot of enamel do to Rachel? Anything? Gretchen knew some of the standard warnings about the chemicals in the compound. Flammable; if exposed wash skin; flush eyes; get medical attention. But would it be enough to incapacitate the mad woman?

Gretchen grabbed the can with her good arm, fought against the pain, used her left hand to remove the cap. She felt as though she might pass out.

She'd never wake up if that happened.

Rachel was above, turning the hammer. She was going to strike her with the sharp end. "You're making this difficult," she said. "If you'd listened to me, you wouldn't be in pain. Mommy didn't feel a thing. I don't want to hurt you, really I don't."

"Wait!" The spray can felt full. Rachel hadn't even noticed. She was focused on her mission. "Let me get up," Gretchen said. "I want to do it your way."

"Yes, that would be best. I can't stand to

see you hurting."

What a crazy woman!

Holding her damaged arm against her body, Gretchen struggled slowly to her feet. As soon as she was upright, Gretchen abruptly turned, raised her good arm, and sprayed Rachel's face without letting up. Rachel screamed and swung the hammer, striking empty air and throwing her off balance. She staggered. Gretchen got in one last blast before running for the stairs.

She felt nauseated by the pain in her shoulder and from the fumes that had filled the air.

Gretchen heard the downstairs door open, saw men with badges below her, felt her knees buckling. "Upstairs," she said.

They pounded past her. One of the officers stayed behind. He bent down to her. "You're going to be okay," he said. "I'm right here."

Shouts came from above. Then a shrill scream.

A cop at the top of the stairs called down. "She jumped from the balcony."

Gretchen leaned against the rail, cradling her arm.

From below she heard other officers talking, shouting orders. She caught enough of what they said to know that her attacker hadn't survived the fall.

This time, Rachel really *was* dead.

The officer who was protecting Gretchen moved aside. Strong, capable arms lifted her.

"Are you all right?"

"What took you so long?" she said to Matt.

"Oh, so now you want me," he said. "It's about time."

He gave her a dazzling smile, but his face was pale and he had that trapped look he got when his doll phobia kicked in.

"Get me out of here," she said.

"Great idea."

55

Home. There really wasn't anyplace like home. Gretchen found herself surrounded by well-wishers and a pack of small animals. Even Wobbles braved the crowd to welcome her. Her arm was in a sling, and pain medication pumped through her veins making her feel warm and mellow. She'd been lucky: only her collarbone was broken. It would heal.

The sexiest man alive sat next to her.

"We're going to call you the aerosol queen," Matt said.

April giggled, watching him with adoring eyes. "The attack of the aerosol queen," she said. "A great name for a movie."

"Quit calling me names," Gretchen said, laughing.

"It's true," Nina said. "You blasted Jerome, then Andy and Julie. You are the aerosol queen."

"I've removed every spray can from the

house," Caroline said.

"Very funny. And I didn't blast Andy."

"You clobbered him," April said. "Good thing you didn't do permanent damage."

Nina was fussing with Tutu's barky braids, straightening them before she said, "What a horrible life Richard had. Committed to an insane asylum when he wasn't unbalanced at all!"

"Like *One Flew Over the Cuckoo's Nest*," April said. "That Nurse Ratched was more nuts than the inmates. It turns out that Rachel was the crazy one in the family."

Gretchen couldn't tear her gaze from Matt. "She was so convincing," she said. "I never would have guessed that Julie had removed her mother's head from the armoire. Her intention was to take her mother's body out, or what was left of it, in bits and pieces." What a gruesome thought.

"We tested her tote bag," Matt said. "She transported Flora Swilling's head inside it."

"Yuck," April said. "And to think I was alone at the museum with her. I bet she took Flora's head that day."

"We discovered the skeleton before she completed her mission," Nina said. "Thanks to our friendly ghost."

Matt's Chrome cologne was acting as an elixir. Gretchen felt light-headed. "What about the real Julie Wicker? Did she exist as Rachel said?"

"Julie Wicker actually was Rachel's second cousin. When the real Julie Wicker passed away, Rachel, always the schemer, sent for her birth certificate and reinvented herself as Julie."

"On a part-time basis?" Gretchen thought this was utterly bizarre.

"Exactly. She was testing out her new role in case she needed it one day. That day came when Allison Thomasia arrived in Phoenix and Rachel thought she had put together too many pieces. Allison began to delve too deeply into their family history and that really set Rachel off."

Nina shivered. "And to think that she was a member of our club, that she was one of the cast members."

Gretchen snuggled closer to Matt. Her shoulder injury had saved her from having to deal with his anger. Instead, he was in male protective mode. She liked it. "Trudy Fernwich came as a big surprise to her."

"Yes, thanks to due diligence by Attorney McNalty, the trustee," Matt said. "Trudy Fernwich is Flora's niece, but she was a black sheep of sorts and hadn't kept in touch with the rest of the family for many years. McNalty is shocked at what happened. Allison came to his office, and, thinking he was doing a good turn, he brought her together with another family member, Julie Wicker. He's understandably upset."

"Andy flew back to LA," Caroline said.

"I was worried that I had killed him." Gretchen felt more than a little guilty about her attacks on two innocent men.

"He'll be fine," Matt said. "And he refused to press charges against you, although I tried to talk him into it." From the playful grin on his face, Gretchen knew he was kidding.

Gretchen glanced at her mother. "I'm glad you didn't marry him. He's not one of my favorite people."

"Andy's been under incredible stress," Caroline said, defending him to the very end.

"Jerome is behind bars for a while," Matt said.

"We aren't pursuing charges against him for entering the museum," Caroline said.

"That will help," Matt said. "But he still has a concealed weapon charge to deal with."

Nimrod leapt at Gretchen's legs until Matt picked him up so he could give Gretchen a kiss.

"I missed you, too," she said.

"What about me?" Matt said. "Didn't you miss me?"

"Bring your face over here," Gretchen said. "I'll show you just how much I missed you."

"Nina," April said, laughing, "tell us how your psychic antennae went so awry? What about, 'The killer must be a man'?"

"I was wrong this time," Nina said, not fazed by her error. "But I'm going to ask our ghost for help figuring out where I went wrong."

"You're kidding," April said.

"Want to help?"

"No way."

"She's waiting for us at the museum," Nina said. "I can feel it."

Caroline laughed. "You're giving up auras and tarot readings to become a ghost hunter?"

"You don't just quit gifts like mine. I'm simply tuning in to another paranormal wavelength."

"I can't help feeling responsible for some of what happened," Gretchen said. "I'm the one who told Julie that Mom was at the museum the morning she tried to run her off the road."

"How could you have known?" Caroline

said. "She's responsible for her actions, not you."

"I should have known when she left Curves to run errands. She was gone from play practice all morning and I never connected —"

"None of us did," April said.

Gretchen wasn't through. She was cleansing her conscience. "I told the cast that the doll head was at our house. Julie was right there, taking it in. If we had been home, who knows what she would have done to us."

"Why did she want the doll head?" April asked, directing the question to Matt.

He shrugged. "We might never know. Maybe in some twisted way she wanted to keep the doll with her mother."

Gretchen leaned back into the warmth of Matt's arms and closed her eyes. She'd beat Nina's tarot card reading, had changed her fate. Others had been ruined, had suffered despair and sorrow, and for that she was sorry.

But those she loved had survived.

At the moment, she was completely pain free.

Life, she decided, couldn't be better.

56

The lights went on to the thunder of applause. The cast took one bow, then another. Bonnie had pulled off her part without a hitch. Nina, after minor complaints, had stepped into Julie's role and had done an amazing job. Jerome, having served ten days in jail, performed magic with the lights.

Mr. B. sat at the back of the room, clapping right along with the rest of them, his unlit pipe tucked between his teeth.

What a huge success the luncheon was. Enough money had rolled in to open the museum and keep it operational for several months. They would easily fulfill the terms of the contract.

One generous benefactor had pledged even more.

The six-foot Barbie looked stunning in the full-length pink gown April created for her. "No cheerleading outfit for Barbie,"

April said with pride. "This is a formal affair."

Daisy came in after the luncheon guests were gone. She wore her purple and red outfit, and her arms were filled with packages. Gretchen gave her a big one-armed hug, still favoring her left shoulder.

"The big day is right around the corner," Gretchen said. "Are you ready?"

"I bought my wedding dress," she said, putting down several enormous shopping bags. "I'll show it to you later."

Gretchen glanced at the bags and was surprised to see that they were from expensive stores. What was going on?

"I have a little money of my own," Daisy said. "I don't usually need it."

"A little? Don't need it?"

"Most of it's in trust."

"In trust?" Gretchen sounded like a parrot, repeating everything her friend said.

"I heard about Rachel and what she tried to do to you," Daisy said. "I feel sorry for the way it ended up. I have some issues of my own, but I'm going to work on them."

Gretchen smiled at her homeless friend. "I think you're wonderful just the way you are."

"I'm sorry that the present I gave you caused so many problems."

"A gift? What?" What had Daisy given her? Love. Loyalty. Friendship. All of those things.

"The museum," Daisy said.

"What about it?"

"I own the house. Well, not really. It will always be part of the family trust, but I get to decide what to do with it. Richard doesn't want to get involved, so we can continue restoring it for a museum."

Gretchen was trying to comprehend. Daisy was their museum benefactor?

"You're Trudy Fernwich? You're the beneficiary?"

Daisy winked. "It's our secret," she said.

"I don't know what to say. I'm speechless."

"Say you'll accept the position of museum curator."

Gretchen sat down at one of the luncheon tables. Fell down, was more like it. The chair saved her from hitting the floor. This couldn't be true. Daisy didn't have twenty dollars to her name.

"What about the repair business?" she stammered. "Mom can't handle it alone."

"She already found a new helper." Daisy adjusted her red hat. "Me. It will be my first paid job. She said you would teach me. Well? What do you say?"

"Why don't you want to run the museum?"

"Me? No. Can you see me meeting with those wealthy people who were here for the luncheon? I don't think so. Besides, it's haunted."

Gretchen's mind was fast at work. She'd bring in traveling doll collections and give presentations. The world of dolls was an endless parade of fashion and history. The traveling doll trunk was in the museum where it belonged. She'd made sure of that. What else would she discover in the storage boxes?

On the sidewalk outside, she saw Matt coming toward her. He hadn't been ready to face a stage full of dolls. They had plenty of time later to overcome his phobia.

Tonight was the night. She was sure of it. The mating dance was about to end.

Then he stopped. Put his cell phone to his ear. Glanced at her. Apologetic eyes.

Gretchen sighed. She'd lost him again.

Nina traipsed past on her way to her Impala. Stopped. Held up a deck of cards between long tapered nails. "Come with me," she said. "The cards don't lie. You suffered pain, did you not? Come. You need a new reading. Where will the future take you next?"

Everything was back to normal.
Whatever that was.

ABOUT THE AUTHOR

Deb Baker collects vintage Barbie dolls and contemporary Zawieruszynski Originals, and can be found haunting doll conventions and shows. Originally an enthusiastic researcher with only two treasured childhood dolls, she is proud to announce that she is irrevocably hooked on dolls and doll collecting.

Visit Deb and her dolls at www.debbaker books.com.

We hope you have enjoyed this Large Print book. Other Thorndike, Wheeler, Kennebec, and Chivers Press Large Print books are available at your library or directly from the publishers.

For information about current and upcoming titles, please call or write, without obligation, to:

Publisher
Thorndike Press
295 Kennedy Memorial Drive
Waterville, ME 04901
Tel. (800) 223-1244

or visit our Web site at:

http://gale.cengage.com/thorndike

OR

Chivers Large Print
published by BBC Audiobooks Ltd
St James House, The Square
Lower Bristol Road
Bath BA2 3SB
England
Tel. +44(0) 800 136919
email: bbcaudiobooks@bbc.co.uk
www.bbcaudiobooks.co.uk

All our Large Print titles are designed for easy reading, and all our books are made to last.